THE SELKIE WHO LOVED A WOLF

SARAH MÄKELÄ

KISSA PRESS LLC

THE SELKIE WHO LOVED A WOLF

CRY WOLF, BOOK 5

Love heals even the deepest wounds...

The wounded werewolf...

After being held in captivity by scientists for months, Colin Fraser needs rest and recuperation. The Scottish Highlands offer him the perfect place to get much-needed distance from the world and repair the bond with his inner beast.

The selkie's search...

Unna Mikkelsen is being urged to mate with a selkie man she doesn't care for. But she'll never forget how, as a young girl, she saw her mother taken by a fisherman. Knowing she must make her peace with the world above the waves, she leaves the deep for dry land—even though this means she's putting herself into danger.

The power of immortal love...

When Colin notices Unna in the pub, he realizes there's more to her than meets the eye. But he fights his feelings for her—how can a wolf as broken as he is have a relationship? Little does he know Unna will need him when her pelt is stolen by a fisherman, causing her to relive her childhood trauma. Or how much he'll need her too, because only her love can heal his wounds…

Sign up for Sarah's newsletter for her latest news, giveaways, excerpts, and much more!
http://bit.ly/SarahMakelaNewsletter

Editor: Word Vagabond

Cover Artist: The Killion Group

ISBN-13: 978-1-942873-83-9

COLIN

*A*lmost a week had passed since the Southeastern Pack had rescued me from that bloody research facility. Memories of being locked in a cage and prodded with needles like some science experiment still haunted me. As much as I tried, my thoughts continually returned to the horror I'd gone through. Chad Fitzroy had been generous to let me leave even though his father, the Pack's Alpha, wanted all available werewolves on guard in case they faced retaliation from whoever was behind that hellhole. From what I'd heard, no one was certain whether the government had led the project or if it had been a group of mad scientists. When I'd been there, they hadn't said much within my hearing. I hadn't really cared who was in charge because I was sure I wouldn't live long enough for it to matter.

My hands trembled as I took another swig of Scotch ale, despite it being seven o'clock in the morning. I'd hoped getting away from the world would make my problems easier to cope with, but I was at my breaking point. Alcohol dulled my pain and lessened my worries. It didn't stop them, though. Every time I closed my eyes, I relived the terror of being locked up in that damned cage. None of this—the alcohol, the stress, the nightmares—helped the incredibly shaky control I had over my wolf. If I didn't regain my composure soon, I feared I would become more beast than man. The scariest part was I'd seen a Pack member go rogue before. The Scottish Pack had killed the wolf to protect our secret, and also to let the beast finally have solace. I pushed those thoughts aside, not wanting to dwell on what could happen if I didn't get my act together.

Silence weighed on the cottage like a thick blanket. My ears perked at each soft sound. The idyllic daydream I'd had of renewing the bond with my beast seemed to drift farther and farther away. How could I relax when it was hard enough to just breathe? For months on end, I'd stayed alert and on edge, always watching and waiting for some bastard in a lab coat to hurt me. Regardless of the distance, I didn't feel much different now. Being away from civilization—for the most part—in the peaceful Scottish Highlands seemed surreal. I wondered if the quiet and calm were worse for my nerves than the bustle of Edinburgh had been.

The cottage I'd rented was a fair bit from the nearest village's sparse population. I'd planned this trip to give me a good shot at taming my beast without too many bystanders. The last thing I needed was to be the reason werewolves were revealed to the world at large. If anyone found out what I was, I'd have to kill them, and if I did, I greatly feared for my humanity. Would my wolf finally take over? Would the Pack...

Fucking stop!

Leaning back in the kitchen chair, I pressed the cool, dark-brown bottle of ale to my forehead, trying to get myself under control. *Deep breaths...* I took a few calming breaths, then gulped down some more ale. My racing heart rate steadied. I placed the bottle back on the table, but I didn't take my hand away from the comfort of its presence.

Coming home to Scotland had been bittersweet. My intention was to spend time reconnecting with my wereleopard half-sister, Caitlyn, as I regained my composure and sanity. But my late father, whom I'd always been told was a good man—and dead—had ruined my plans. *Bloody monster.* That had pushed me over the edge, but I gained a new respect for my sister, knowing the pain she'd been through as a wee lass at his hands. She'd put on a brave face to protect me, but I couldn't help feeling a little betrayed. Either she or our mother should've been honest with me. Instead, they'd let me spend most of my life loving some woman-abusing arsehole. My hand trembled around the bottle.

Leaving Caitlyn in her weakened condition was brutal, but if I'd stayed, I would have put the Scottish Pack—and most importantly, her—at risk. I didn't like feeling as if I would snap at any given moment. My fragile control over my beast left me vulnerable, especially with all that had happened recently. When I was in Edinburgh, my focus had been solely on keeping my sister safe. I refused to let her see how torn apart I was now. Dougal's passionate glances told me he'd try to protect her, but the lass had no idea what she'd gotten herself into by falling for the Alpha.

I clenched my hands into fists, and the bottle of Scotch ale shattered. Pain bit my palm as alcohol seeped into the wounds. Opening my fist, I frowned at the large shard of brown glass protruding from my skin. *Shite, what a waste of perfectly good ale.*

Crimson blood mixed with ale and dripped onto the floor. If I didn't take care of the mess, the cottage's owner might think to ask questions about my stay. This needed to be cleaned straight away. My hand didn't worry me all that much. It'd be fine. With my supernatural healing, I'd survived a hell of a lot worse.

If only that healing helped my mind...

I cupped my wounded hand to my chest palm-up to try to slow the bleeding, then stepped over the broken glass in my now-damp socks to reach the kitchen sink. The window's distant seaside view, with its jagged cliffs and sweeping waves, struck pride in my heart, and I remembered again just why I'd come back to my homeland. Caitlyn and I had visited a place not far from here for some time as kids. It'd been one of my favorite memories as a young lad. Our mother kept us on the move growing up, never settling down for long. Now I knew why.

The ache in my hand tugged me back to the present. Yanking the large piece of glass from my palm wouldn't be fun, but it needed to be done. The skin around the wound was already trying to heal. If I didn't get the glass out soon, it would hurt much more than it did now. The shard was buried deep, nearly penetrating all the way through to the other side. If I were human, I'd have needed immediate medical attention.

I firmly pinched the glass with the hem of my shirt, between my thumb and index finger. My grip on the sharp shard slipped the first time, but on the second try, I jerked the fragment out of my hand, leaving a long gash behind. A new rush of agony ripped at my palm. Blood poured from the wound, no longer held back by the glass. I held my hand over the sink, letting the drain drink the thick red liquid as I searched the nearby cupboards for a first-aid kit. The kit was rather dusty, but it contained plenty of gauze to wrap the wound.

The chunk of glass had come out fairly smoothly, so I wasn't worried about any fragments getting left behind in my hand. My lycanthropy would likely push the foreign object from my body anyway, as it had done with a bullet once. I'd been a stupid teenager who thought more about impressing a female werewolf than keeping an eye out for an old farmer protecting his livestock. I learned my lesson. Particularly since, as punishment, I'd been locked for a full month and a half in the same cage where Caitlyn had been held.

I turned on the faucet, rinsing the open wound before I patted it dry with a formerly white towel that hung on a hook by the sink. I'd do what I could to clean it up, but I wasn't very domesticated. Tasks like that were a bit outside my area of expertise. Maybe the towel would just 'go missing.' I'd rather that than have the owner see it stained.

Once I'd wrapped the wound with a respectable amount of gauze, I opened the cupboard below the sink to inspect what cleaning agents the owner provided her tenants. I needed something that could clean up the blood and ale that had spilled all over the floor. I grabbed the bleach and set it on the counter. The scent hit my nostrils like a boxer's right hook, my mind flashing back to the overwhelming scent I'd endured at the laboratory. Panic rose within me like a massive wave. I stumbled away from the counter, slipped on the blood and booze, and fell on my arse.

The world faded away.

Bars surrounded me, and I let out a low snarl of displeasure in my wolf form. Two men stood outside of the cage where I was kept, with a young woman draped over the taller, bald man's shoulder. Not even my supernatural strength could help me break free from this laboratory. I'd tried many times, but the bars were too sturdy. Fury tore through me at the fact that these people were in my room. They didn't look like scientists, so I doubted they were supposed to be here. My beast lingered near the surface of my human skin. We were fast becoming one and the same, and I feared for my humanity.

The bald man slid his hands up the woman's legs until they reached her thighs. From this angle, I could tell she wore nothing under her denim skirt. My pulse raced, and my libido revved up. The moon would be full tonight, and werewolves were driven to uncontrollable cravings for sex during the days surrounding the full moon, with the peak night being the most severe. I slid my tongue over my lips. We wanted a warm, feminine body beside us.

Anger pulsed through my veins as the bald man started to reach higher. My wolf wanted me to act, to claim what had to be ours.

The skinny man with glasses who accompanied him cleared his throat. "Brad, that's not appropriate. Just..." He glanced in my direction, but I knew he couldn't see me. This section of the cage was dark. A couple lights had been broken during a prior mishap, and I'd made their lives hell the few times they'd tried to fix them. The predator in me knew how to cloak us very well. "Let's get this over with." The man took a few steps back, blood pounding through his veins in a quick staccato.

My jaws ached to clench over his throat and drink the adrenaline pulsing through him.

It had been weeks since I'd last tasted meat, and my body desperately needed the protein. The idea of eating someone usually wouldn't cross my mind, and the fact that it came to me now was horrifying. I battled with my wolf, pleading with him to stop marching down that path, but he wouldn't listen. After all, he was only trying to survive. We turned our anger on the intruders.

The bald man slid the young woman down his body in front of the bars. Her head, with its long, dark brown hair, slumped toward her chest. She wore only a bra and the denim skirt. Her slow, slightly labored breathing told me she'd been knocked out with the same drugs they'd used on me. However, her scent told me she wasn't a shapeshifter. He grabbed a pair of long gloves from the side table the scientist and his helpers used when they tried to handle me. They thought the reinforced gloves would protect them from an attack and prevent them from being turned into another

6

guinea pig for this laboratory, but they were wrong. I could rip through the gloves and infect them. I'd just not tried very hard. Yet.

I lowered myself toward the ground in a crouch, ready to pounce on the man at the first opportunity. The change rolled over me almost like magic. The pain and discomfort were minimal. It usually hurt a lot, but I'd gotten excellent at shifting to my wolf form during my time here, perhaps due to my beastly nature coming closer to the surface. Going back to human form...now that hurt.

My tail swished back and forth in agitation as I waited for the moment to act.

The girl coughed and slowly moved her head to the side. She was still dazed and hadn't yet come out of her drug-induced state, but her movements made me tense. I struggled with my lust and the need to destroy. The man grabbed her by the upper arms and hoisted her back against the bars. I snarled again, giving them a final warning to leave.

The bald man stared over the woman's shoulder as he pushed her firmly against the cage as if she were a sacrificial virgin to be given to a monster. His complexion went pure white, and he kept as much distance as he could between himself and the cage.

The beast within me grew ever more anxious and ready to attack. He was our target. We wanted to sate our lust with the girl, not kill her.

She struggled with the bald man, and I could taste her fear on my tongue like sweet honey. "Let me go, you arse—"

I charged forward, lashing out before I could contain myself. My claws aimed for the man's arm, but the lass cried out in anguish instead. The warm scent of her blood chilled me to the core, breaking the wolf's firm hold on my mind. I retreated back to the darkened corner, fully knowing the damage I'd caused.

I had given them exactly what they wanted. Now this girl would suffer from my mistake for the rest of her miserable life.

Blinking my eyes open, I groaned at the sharp pain

radiating through the back of my head. My hand shook as I pressed my fingers against it to see more blood. Fucking shite. I glanced over my shoulder to double-check the cupboard I'd hit to make sure it was still intact. Werewolves were well known for their hard-headedness.

Thankfully, it was.

I carefully climbed to my feet, making sure I didn't slip again. Those haunting memories were the reason I barely slept anymore. I didn't need to knock myself unconscious again to further relive them.

The kitchen floor was slick with Scotch ale, broken glass, and an unhealthy amount of blood. I mopped up the mess I'd smeared across the floor, before showering and changing clothes. That bottle of ale had been the last one in the house, and with how raw my nerves were getting, a few pints at the pub for lunch might not be a bad idea. If alcohol was the key to soothing my beast, then that's what I'd use to heal my pain and repair our bond.

2

UNNA

$\mathcal{M}$any years had passed since the last time I'd walked amongst humans. Being on land was thrilling, and Scotland's quaint coastal villages deeply interested me. The only trouble I'd run into so far was remembering how to walk on two feet again, but I thought I'd finally gotten the hang of it. I stared down at my toes and wiggled them, unable to get over the cheerful sight of the tiny digits. A smile crept across my lips as I looked around the small cottage's single bedroom.

The people on land were quite friendly, much happier than I remembered them. Times seemed to have changed, and this wasn't the country I'd traveled to before. Perhaps that also contributed to it. My mother had felt it necessary for our people to get away from the sea's depths every so often. She'd brought me on land to fully experience life and acquaint myself with the world beyond the waves. We had visited the beautiful Faroe Islands together.

However, I enjoyed these people farther south. The Scots. They were much jollier, and the climate was a little warmer than the Faroe Islands. Plus, I couldn't bring myself to go back there. Not after...

Don't let your thoughts go there.

Shivering, I wrapped my arms around my stomach and took a few deep breaths to calm myself. The small bedroom around me was pleasant and filled with the modest comforts of land. My fellow selkies had bought the place with the gold and precious human treasures we'd found underwater. By human standards, it still seemed rather cozy, but I didn't mind one bit. I was just happy to be here on land.

My stomach rumbled, and I pressed my hands to my belly. Life as a human was such an adventure. I slid off the mattress to gently place my seal pelt in the hefty storage chest at the end of the bed. I marveled at the intricate design of a sea maiden on it before locking my pelt away with a sturdy padlock about the size of my palm. If anyone found my sealskin, I'd...

Stop it!

But my thoughts drifted back to my mother before I could wrest them under control. While we'd been in the Faroe Islands, we didn't have anywhere to store our pelts like this. We saw the islands during the day and slept under the stars near the beach at night. We had tucked our pelts beneath two good-sized rocks by the shore. A fisherman came upon my mother's sealskin and stole it. When we traveled back for them at the end of our trip, he took her away while I hid behind a rock. That had been the first and only time I'd felt true terror in my life. Nothing I could've done would have saved her. I'd been so small and alone, huddled on the beach as the days passed. She returned to the beach on the third day and sent me back to the sea where my father could protect me. He'd been furious with himself for letting us go, because no matter how long or how hard he searched, my mother was never seen again. He hadn't been the same since that day.

Tears trailed down my cheeks, and I wiped at the moisture as I perched on the large chest. *Let it go.* If I couldn't move past those memories, I'd just flee back to the water. It had taken so much time and effort to convince my father to let me make this trip, to reassure him that I'd be fine on land again. To go back to the water this soon would be throwing that all away. This was a chance for me to prove to myself that I wasn't a victim anymore. Besides, it had been many years since one of our people had gone missing on land. We'd grown smarter when it came to handling humans, and it didn't hurt that stories of us had faded from popular consciousness. We were creatures of folklore and fairy tales now.

Durness, Scotland, had many things I wanted to see. The beach had a cave I'd seen so many times from the sea. The site attracted plenty of people. Another local hotspot, according to one of the selkies in my pod, was the pub where humans gathered around to eat, drink, and gossip. My stomach growled again at the thought of sampling human food. The pub was a little ways off by walking, but I didn't mind trying out my legs and feet. The excitement of being on land still left me a little breathless.

---

*B*y the time I reached the pub, my feet ached and dizziness threatened to topple me over. The trip had taken longer and had been more exhausting than I'd first imagined. Maybe I should've called Ailsa, the human caretaker of our pod's cottage, and asked for a ride. She always told my people that we were more than welcome to come to her when we needed help. My mother had trusted her as a friend when the pod purchased the house, and she took good care of us when we were on land like we were her own children.

I leaned against the side of a small grocery store across from the pub and focused on taking deep breaths. It surprised me to feel this sore so soon, but perhaps it took time to acclimate to human form. Seals didn't walk several kilometers for food. We glided through the water after our prey. Just thinking about hunting made me even more famished.

I pushed away from the grocery store and crossed the parking lot to the pub. A large group of people crowded inside as I approached, especially for a village this size. My mother had told me humans ate lunch around this time, which probably explained my rampant hunger. A bell chimed over my head as I entered. Behind the bar, an older man nodded his head to me and smiled. Unless I wanted to squeeze between two large gentlemen at the bar, the only vacant table was near a group of rowdy men who spoke in loud, lilting voices. My mother had taught me several languages growing up, but I couldn't understand what these men were saying. I tried listening in despite myself, but they had to be speaking Scottish Gaelic. I shook my head, dismissing the attempt, and sat at the table.

A few of the boisterous men glanced in my direction. They appeared to be in their late thirties, and a decent bit older than the early twenties my human form looked. One of the men grinned at me. The gesture lit up his ruddy face, brightening his clear blue eyes.

Why were they staring at me? Had I done something wrong? Maybe I'd shown signs of my otherness. I smiled back, but my heart pounded in my chest.

Father had allowed me to come on land, but his one restriction was that I keep to myself at all times and not engage any humans. Losing me might kill him, especially since his true soulmate was gone. He'd taken another selkie wife to continue our kind, but his once-glowing happiness had been replaced by an aura of grief and sorrow. All the joy I'd known and loved about him had been stolen away with my mother.

The men around the ruddy-faced guy laughed and gave him a playful shove in my direction, but he remained firmly planted in his chair. He turned to them and spoke in a low, terse voice.

The bell chimed as a new patron strode through the pub's doors. Something drew my gaze toward him. He was tall, with curly red hair, and exuded a feral power like nothing I'd ever witnessed before. My people had three predators: killer whales, sharks, and humans. He felt a lot scarier than any of them. Fear raked her claws down the length of my spine, and I sat up straighter. White gauze bound his hand as if he'd been recently injured. *An injured predator is a dangerous one.*

The ruddy-faced Scot tapped my shoulder, nearly making me tumble from my chair. "Is this seat taken?" he said with another toothy smile. He spoke slowly and enunciated carefully as if he'd rightly guessed that I might not have understood him and his friends. That made me wonder what they'd been saying to him, but it wasn't my biggest concern. Not with the pub's newcomer drawing my attention.

The tall man sat on the barstool I'd declined, and ordered some sort of amber ale, which the bartender put before him in a pint glass. *Is he dangerous? Should I leave?*

No, he hadn't even looked in my direction during the short time he'd been here. Perhaps I was just nervous from all the aching thoughts of my mother's fate. I refused to just leave. As long as I blended in with the crowd and didn't draw attention to myself, I'd be fine. After I experienced life on land, I had to return home to the sea and the arms of my promised mate, Ægir. My father knew I didn't want to be with him, but we had made a deal. If I came on this trip, I wouldn't fight his choice for my betrothal tooth and flipper. Little did I know who he'd choose. The thought made me crave one of the pub's alcoholic drinks.

The man at my side placed his hand on my shoulder, completely dragging me from my thoughts.

I whipped around to face him. My sensitive nerves were making me jumpy. It had been a long time since anyone touched me. After losing my mother and seeing my father's pain, I'd kept my distance, unwilling to go through more hurt. Yet I rather liked the sensation, even if I wasn't sure about this stranger doing it. Human customs were still new to me, but something about the action felt possessive.

Frowning, he let his hand drop to his side. "Are ye all right? You seem quite startled, lass." He narrowed his eyes at the red-haired man at the bar, and for a moment, I thought I caught a whiff of jealousy. How silly. Maybe I'd imagined it.

"Yes, I'm fine. Sorry." I lowered my gaze to the table. A wave of anxiety hit me, and I wasn't as comfortable being there at the pub anymore. Between the man at the bar and this guy trying to get my attention, my emotions were beginning to overwhelm me. If I borrowed the phone, Ailsa could come pick me up. She'd always said she didn't mind providing for us while we were on land. "Perhaps I should leave."

"Nonsense. You haven't had anything to eat yet, and you're looking mighty thin." He ran his gaze over me, and his smile grew remarkably brighter. "You're not from around here, are you? I haven't heard that particular accent before."

I opened my mouth to summon a response, but no words came out. He knew I was different. What could I say to dissuade him? My mother had taught me many languages, but we weren't from any particular area. We were drifters, and we didn't speak human languages amongst our own kind. Our accents were quite different, even if we used their languages. When we wore our sealskins, we were wild and free. My mother had been masterful at masking her otherworldliness, but this man's over-the-top desire for my attention caused me to falter.

The intensity of my hunger had long since faded. Dread roiled my stomach instead. I rose to my feet even as my belly growled in protest at leaving the delicious-smelling human food. "Sorry, I really should be leaving."

The ruddy-faced man's friends from the other table waved their arms at us and raised their raucous voices at him in Gaelic. He slapped the table hard, drawing several looks from other patrons. He snapped at them in a harsh tone.

My heart skipped a beat at the loud exchange. I didn't even try listening in this time. More than ever, I wanted to return to the sanctuary of my pod's cottage.

"Lass, please." He snaked his arm around my waist, and he pulled me back into a chair beside him. "I apologize for coming across so strong. We didn't mean to make you uncomfortable. If you really don't want me to bother you, I can go back to my mates. Just stay." His tone softened, and he looked wholly repentant. Not at all like a predator, unlike the man at the bar.

I still wasn't comfortable here, but if I left now, that might seem suspicious. Another lesson my mother had taught me: keep calm and pretend to be human while on land. If you act like something other than human, they'll know, and bad things will happen. The fact that she was gone forever proved that.

A shiver of revulsion chased down my spine at having this man's hands on my waist so intimately, but I did as he said. "Okay, I'll stay." I glanced over to the redheaded man at the bar again. My heart skipped a beat as he stared back at us…at me. Sweat slicked my palms, and I rubbed them against my pants, returning my attention to the gentleman on my right. *Stay calm, be human, and keep it together.* Once I had lunch, I'd head back to the cottage. Everything would be okay if I did as I was trained. I did *not* want to end up being abducted like my mother.

3

COLIN

*A*lmost as soon as I set foot inside the pub, I sensed someone watching me. My wolf paced just under the surface of my skin, growling at me to let him out, but right now would be the worst time to do that. The Scotch ale barely helped soothe my frazzled nerves. I could likely drink water and get the same result. The friendly old Scottish bartender, Mike Melville, distracted me a bit, but I was beginning to regret coming out to the pub. Perhaps I should've gone to the shops instead. At least then I'd be able to enjoy the ale without being gawked at, let alone all the noise from the rowdy group speaking Scottish Gaelic. The occasional raucous laughter brought back memories I was trying, with little success, to drown.

A pale young lass with blonde hair the color of wheat glanced in my direction every few moments. Was she mad? Yet something in her blue eyes drew me in. I didn't bother myself with one-night stands, unless they were necessitated by the full moon, especially now when I couldn't guarantee my self-restraint. Any woman—human or wolf—would find herself in danger in my bed.

Not that it mattered much. She already appeared to have a companion. Never mind that she kept leaning away from him. Her suitor's friends, at a nearby table, jeered and taunted the man...Murray, I think...in Gaelic, cajoling him into not letting the lass off so easily. Prove himself to be a man. Murray cursed at them, saying he was much manlier than they were, but their prodding seemed to bolster his courage to convince the lass to stay. Something about that group unsettled my wolf. Maybe he found them too similar to the mercenaries at the science lab, with their excessive arrogance.

The lass's suitor guided her back into a chair with his hand on her waist. She glanced back at me, but quickly averted her gaze as if surprised I'd noticed her. I couldn't miss the nervous look in her sea-blue eyes. The man at her side glared at me, jealousy rearing its ugly head, but I wasn't impressed. I could easily snap his thick neck... *Quiet these thoughts, man. You don't need any trouble.*

No one else paid the couple too much attention. Maybe they knew how this man was, but I'd keep an eye out to make sure no unwanted behavior went on, if I could. I'd had enough of women being abused. While I wouldn't involve myself unnecessarily, I couldn't stand by and let it happen.

The woman looked thin, and I almost thought I heard her stomach growl softly through the general pub noise. It seemed as if she hadn't eaten in a while. The way she drew me in, I almost wondered if there was more to her than met the eye. I didn't think she was another werewolf or feline shifter, because I didn't feel much power wafting off her. But all the people and the smell of food wafting through the place distracted my nose, so I couldn't be sure. It didn't really matter. I wasn't here on Pack business, and I wanted nothing to do with those politics now.

I turned to the bar, resettling into drinking away my

problems: the terrifying memories of being locked away and helpless, plus the trauma of finding out my sister was abused by my father, and that I'd known the man for years. She was brave for moving on with her life, despite what the foul bastard had done. The only problem lay in the fact she was getting on with the Scottish Pack's Alpha. I didn't like that very much at all. He took care of her, but their relationship couldn't last. The Pack would never accept her, not with the way many werewolves hated those outside our own species. Some wolves would gladly accept being the only type of shifters in existence. Combined with the reserved nature of my fellow Scots, any outsiders at all tended to cause unwanted tension in the ranks.

Sooner or later, I'd need to travel back to the United States to re-join my new Pack. When that time came, I wouldn't be around to protect her. While we hadn't been close before my abduction, the fact that she'd dropped everything in her life to come to my aid truly made me appreciate her. I think I would've done the same for her, but I sincerely hoped we never had to find out.

I'd rather she remain safe. She'd been through enough. I wouldn't move back to the States until I knew she'd be fine with the Scottish Pack, but staying with her right now hadn't been an option. My beast was too unruly, and I wouldn't put her at risk.

The mirror behind the bar showed that the lass and her suitor had settled down at the table. Maybe it was just as well. I didn't have any business getting familiar with women now. Besides, the lass appeared a wee bit too skittish for my wolf. We might not have the patience required for that one, even on our better days.

The ales went down one by one, and just as I started getting a mediocre buzz, the bartender came over. Mike ran his gaze over me, making a show of sizing me up. "Aye, lad, while I'm sure ye can handle them, I'll have to cut ye off. You're a nice fellow. Drinking isn't the answer to your problems, ye ken? I've been there. Perhaps if a good lass cheered ye up, you'd feel better. It doesn't take a blind man to see you've been eyeing that sweet blonde one over there."

Sighing, I leaned in a little. "While I appreciate the concern, I come from hearty stock. Alcohol takes a while to affect me." That much was entirely true. If I ever fell into a vat of ale, I could probably drink my way out all right. Maybe I'd even get drunk off me arse. But I knew having a few pints wasn't doing it. They just dulled the throbbing ache in my chest and my head.

Perhaps he was right, though. Even though I wouldn't succumb to liver disease or other problems related to alcoholism, it further dulled my connection with my beast and widened the gap between us. I was only hurting my attempt to rehabilitate myself and my wolf. My beast needed to know *I* was in charge of my mind, body, and spirit. Neither he nor the alcohol should claim that position. We couldn't be reactionary anymore.

Mike just cocked an eyebrow at me, not looking the least bit convinced.

I spoke up before he could lecture me more. "While we're at it then, I appreciate the attempt at hooking me up, but the lass appears to be taken." Even I doubted they were an item, though. The female appeared more intent on her food than the man she was with.

He wrinkled his nose and looked ready to spit. "Nae, those lads are nothing but trouble. They come here each day at lunch and always cause a ruckus. If ye dinnae want to talk with her, I understand. Just...be kind to yourself. No one else will." He waited a moment to see if his words would sink in and I'd become a changed man, but I just stared at him. He shook his head.

Behind me, Murray lowered his voice as he talked with the woman. He slid his hand along her shoulder and down her arm. She didn't appear to notice his advances, but that didn't stop him from trying.

Two of Murray's friends came up to the bar and stood to either side of me. The men who had been there had left after finishing their food and drinks. The place was starting to empty out a little. These men set me on edge. I could tell they were trouble, and I didn't like being surrounded by them. My hackles rose, but I did my best to remain relaxed, instead of hunching my shoulders and snarling at them the way my wolf wanted to.

The rowdier of the two men waved his hand at the old bartender, who had walked off moments before to handle some newly arrived patrons.

"Hold your horses," the bartender said, shaking his grey head and returning his attention to his customers.

The other man leaned over and reached behind the counter for the bottle of whisky. "If the old man won't serve us, we'll just serve ourselves," he muttered under his breath.

I didn't want any trouble, but my patience was running thin. I wouldn't sit by and let Mike be treated like this by these idiots. I grabbed the thief's wrist. "Wait yer turn."

The rowdy man who had tried calling the bartender over turned to us. "Keep your hands to yourself, stranger. You're not from around here, and I think ye need to be leaving if ye want to remain upright." He towered over me, closing in as if getting in my personal space would force me to release his friend. I would *not* hide under a rock with my tail tucked between my legs for them. These fools had another think coming if they thought I could be so easily intimidated.

Not long ago I'd faced down my own werewolf father with the help of my Alpha, who had—unfortunately—killed the bastard before I could. The thought made me clench my hand, causing the thief to yelp in pain. "Ye and your friends need to run along. Or else I'll alert the bartender to what this one was trying to do." I nodded to the bottle, still in the thief's hand. I think he was simply too afraid to move for fear of what I might do to his wrist.

I wasn't in the mood for any of this.

My beast was rearing for a fight. If he took over now, we'd be done for. The Pack wouldn't allow me to live if I showed the world that werewolves existed.

The loudmouth glanced between me and his friend. He looked foolhardy, like he wouldn't back down regardless of the potential harm to his friend. His eyes were bright with the desire to fight. If this had been any other time, I'd have been glad to give him exactly that, but my control was hanging on by a thread right now. Finally, he seemed to register the pain in his friend's face. "Let him go, and we won't have a problem."

The fact that he relented so easily stirred up my suspicions, but I shrugged it off. I released the man's wrist.

The thief pulled his arm to his chest. His hand was slightly reddish-purple from a lack of blood flow. Maybe I'd been holding on tighter than I'd thought. These two had to have learned their lesson. All I wanted was peace and quiet here, not to be worrying about rural thugs when I was supposed to be recuperating from my months in hell.

Mike glanced over in our direction after the older couple he was serving gestured toward us. He frowned, quietly telling them to give him a moment before heading over. "Is everything all right here?" he asked. No one was quick to shed any light on the subject.

The loudmouth nodded after a minute. "Angus and I were just leaving." He tossed down a few bills for their tab before heading off to the rest of their friends at the table. They spoke in hushed voices, but my Scotch Gaelic was too rusty to know what they were saying. Murray returned to the table and glanced over at me with a grimace on his face. He and the blonde girl had finished their meals, and he'd been talking with her while she nodded occasionally and did her best to shrink back into the chair.

Perhaps she had finally realized that the way his hand was running over her was sexual. She appeared quite naïve for a girl in her early twenties. I turned away, not wanting to think much more about her, but I couldn't stop myself from staring at them through the mirror.

Murray cast a nasty glance my way as he ushered the lass to her feet and then followed his friends to the pub's exit with her in tow. My beast stretched toward the surface of our skin, angry and impatient. We didn't like them being out of our sight. Something about her intrigued us, even if I didn't trust myself with her.

Mike tapped the counter to reclaim my attention. "You should've talked with her when you had the chance, lad. It appears she's off with those hooligans now." His frown deepened. "I think you know exactly what was going on here with those men, too." He leaned in a little closer and lowered his voice so his other customers wouldn't hear.

Perhaps my time had come to pay up and leave before I had to explain my role in it. "Keep an eye on your liquor when they're around." I jerked my head toward to the bottle the thief had tried to snatch, then dug through my wallet. My tab was higher than I'd anticipated, but I left a good tip. Maybe my drinking habit would be detrimental after all...to my pocketbook, at least.

He sighed and shook his head, sadness slumping his shoulders as if he knew exactly what I'd meant. "Have a good one. Stay out of trouble, and I'll see you back here tomorrow."

Embarrassment warmed my cheeks. Was I really that

predictable? Without a word, I nodded and left. When I walked into the fresh seaside air, the troublemakers had already dispersed. The only sign of them came from the faint scent of exhaust. From the mix of it, I could guess they had left in separate vehicles. I only hoped the girl was more capable of handling herself than I thought.

4

UNNA

*T*he one good thing to come from visiting the pub was the delicious food filling my stomach. It would've been nice to enjoy my lunch in peace, but the man I'd met there didn't take no for an answer. Even when it came time to go, he'd insisted on taking me home and all but placed me inside his white pick-up truck. I wondered if that had something to do with the trouble his pals had caused at the bar with the mysterious stranger, but I hardly had room to think with this man's mouth moving almost the entire time we'd been together. It seemed like he enjoyed hearing the sound of his own voice. Throughout the meal, I'd kept my focus on my food while sneaking glances at the red-haired man at the bar.

He'd kept my dinner companion's friends from stealing, and he seemed as interested in my presence as I was in his. My curiosity ramped up, even as fear stirred in my chest. I didn't understand who—or what—he was, but that didn't matter now. The comforts of my people's cottage awaited me. Who knew? I might not even see him again. That idea didn't thrill me, though. Did I *want* to see him again? I frowned at the direction my thoughts were headed as I stared out at the rolling Scottish countryside.

"I hoped you enjoyed the lunch, lass," said the man driving me. "Actually, I haven't caught your name." He chuckled and shook his head. "My apologies. Guess our conversation kept me too busy for normal pleasantries."

I opened my mouth to say my real name, but it was too unusual to human ears. My mother had given me a human name the last time I'd seen her on the Faroe Islands, and I wracked my brain to remember it. "Unna," I said at last. "My name is Unna."

"Exotic. I'm Murray. Much plainer than yours. I figured you weren't from around here. Must be why I haven't heard your accent before, Unna." He grinned at me before pulling into the gravel driveway of my people's cottage. "This must've been quite a walk for a young lass like yourself. I'd be happy to see you again. Maybe if you need another ride, I could show you the sights." He hopped out of the truck before I could respond.

My father had insisted that I not mingle with humans. This didn't feel like a good idea, but I couldn't blow him off. He might become suspicious.

Murray opened the car door, and I jumped a little. He'd given me no real reason to be nervous about being alone with him. I wasn't very comfortable in his presence, but he was fairly kind. He'd paid for my meal and told me about the area, and himself...in detail. There wasn't any reason to think he'd guess what I was and steal me away like the fisherman who had taken my mother.

Besides, my time on land wouldn't last forever. I should just enjoy the experience while it lasted. Sooner or later, I'd have to return to the sea. Even now, my body craved the feeling of cool water sliding over my flippers.

I climbed out of the truck, then headed up the stone path to the cottage's front door. When I turned around to wave after unlocking it, I yelped and pressed a hand over my chest. Murray stood right in front of me. I had to crane my neck to look at his face. My heart raced as I struggled to regain my composure. I flashed him a shaky smile. "Well, I guess it's good-bye." Only now did I notice the way he towered over me, his stature much broader and taller than my own. I pushed down my discomfort, feeling more like prey now. *Stop it!* He'd shown me kindness, nothing else.

"So soon, lass?" He glanced over the top of my head into the cottage. "It's quite a drive back to work. Might I come inside for a cup of coffee first?"

My mouth flapped open and closed. I didn't want to be rude, especially after him saving me the walk. My feet did still ache a little from visiting the pub. And I'd never ridden in an automobile before. That had been kind of exciting. A new experience to share with the others about my stay here on land. Of course, I might need to amend my tale a little so my father wouldn't yell at me.

Stepping back from the doorway, I let Murray inside. "I have tea, but no coffee."

Nodding, he brushed past me. "I'll take a cup if you don't mind." He strolled through the small living area, looking around as if he owned the place. Maybe I shouldn't have been surprised at his brazen behavior, but I was suddenly glad I'd closed the bedroom door when I'd left. When he'd finished with his tour, he sat at the round kitchen table. "Nice little place you've got here."

I smiled, pleased with the compliment. My people took great pride in our humble abode. It was good to know a human saw its charming qualities too. "Thank you." I went to the stove and put some water to boil in the kettle. That much I did know about making tea, but most of this situation was unfamiliar to me. Maybe his being here wasn't so bad after all. Perhaps my nervousness was fear of adventure, nothing more.

One thing I did know was that if I didn't get myself under control, he might become suspicious. There was no telling what humans knew about selkies. Most these days weren't well-versed in mythology, so the potential for them believing in my kind had greatly lessened. But not all discounted the old tales, especially in this region, which made life harder on us.

He watched me closely from his spot at the table, his gaze lazily sliding from the top of my head to my toes and back again. "So what's a nice lass like yourself doing here in Durness all alone?"

"Just visiting. Scotland is a beautiful country." I pulled a couple of tea bags from the cupboard, doing what I could to busy myself while he stared at me. His persistent gaze troubled me.

"You'll be going home after your visit? To the Faroe Islands?"

I nodded, unable to trust my voice, afraid it might show how much he was unnerving me. I didn't like all these questions. The instinct rose within me to evade this predator, clenching my throat like a vise.

"What's it like there, Unna?" He came up behind me, blocking me in the tiny kitchen so I wouldn't be able to leave without bumping into him.

"Breathtaking. Peaceful. Lots of green grass and mountains." I'd only been once as a human, and that had been many years ago. My last memory was of being taken back to the sea by my broken father, who couldn't bear my mother's disappearance. Sadness squeezed my chest, and I wanted to cry at the thought. *Be strong.*

"Maybe I'll look you up if I ever make it over there." Murray took a few steps toward me, and I leaned away, bumping into the counter, unable to stop myself. The sharp whistle of the tea kettle sounded behind me, and I jumped. "You're pretty skittish, aren't you?" He tossed back his head and laughed. I slid past him and turned off the stove before pouring the water into the cups I'd set out on the counter top.

"Sorry. I guess I'm still tired from all the traveling." That much was true. I'd swum all last night without stop to make it here. I'd been eager to start my first day among humans, and now it was upon me. So much of my energy had been spent by my excitement…and negative emotions. It was now barely midday, and I was more than ready to take a nap, but there was so much to do and see.

"It's understandable. Traveling can do that." He held up the tea bag, then glanced at me with regret in his eyes. "Actually, I can't stay. I need to head back to work. Let's get to know one another better while you're here. I can take you to see the sights. There are many, and walking won't get you far."

"Yes, I guess that's true." I'd planned on slipping into my pelt for any longer distances, but that could be risky with all the humans I'd seen wandering the beaches. There was Ailsa, but Murray seemed relatively harmless, if a little overwhelming. Then again, I wasn't used to human men.

I walked him to the door, and he turned to me on the porch. "I look forward to seeing you again, Unna. You're a sweet little lass." He pulled a pen from his pocket and a crumpled piece of paper. "Ring me when you'd like to see the sights."

"Okay." Smiling, I shut the door behind him. I looked down at the long number he'd written on the slip of paper and cocked my head to the side. This had to be one of those telephone numbers I'd heard of. I rose to my tiptoes to peek outside the door's window as Murray started the engine on his truck and pulled out of the driveway.

Maybe adventure was just what I needed before my father tethered me to a selkie husband.

5

COLIN

*T*he three six-packs of beer I'd picked up on the way home sat beside me on the quaint porch. The clear blue sky overhead never ceased to amaze me, nor did the distant waves against the shore. My body relaxed a little, and I leaned back on my elbows. The blonde girl from the pub kept fluttering through my thoughts. The naïveté in her eyes was like nothing I'd ever seen before. Very different from my sister Caitlyn. The girl was almost otherworldly, and I couldn't help feeling responsible for her leaving with those rowdy men. Dread filled my stomach.

If anything happened to her, I'd only have myself to blame. Mike knew the group better than I, and he had nudged me in her direction, but my stubbornness had kept me from acting. My wild needs were placed above all others. Again.

I slapped my palms against the hardwood beneath me. There was nothing I could do now. I didn't know where she was staying, so I couldn't check on her. Besides, if I did look for her and find her, she might find my presence strange. My only hope remained that she wasn't as helpless as she looked.

While drinking wasn't the answer to my many problems, perhaps it would do for now. Mike thought he knew me, but he was wrong. He only knew the man I portrayed, not the savage beast beneath my skin. When the sun set, I'd work on my bond with my wolf. Until then, I wanted nothing more than to dull the brutal pain in my chest and head, and remain human for as long as I could.

What would my mum think of my alcoholic behavior? Let alone Caitlyn... I'd left her injured and suffering, going off to heal my own wounds instead of looking after her in her time of need. I was a bloody bastard.

Clenching my fists, I rose to my feet. The cottage was nice, but I didn't want to hang out here too much, not with the mood I was in. The fewer questions my landlady had when I returned the keys, the better. I'd yet to travel to the beach. Perhaps seeing some of the local sights would help clear my thoughts.

After setting the beer in the fridge, I locked up the cottage. My wolf yearned to run as fast as we could, but I couldn't chance anyone spotting my beast, so I kept my pace to a sprint. It took a little while to get to the beach, but it was more than worth it. Surprisingly, I felt calmer after the run. The waves crashing against the rocks lulled me into a relaxation I hadn't felt in a long time, and the crisp sea air revitalized a part of me that I hadn't known was hurting. People roamed around here and there. I took off my shoes and socks, heading off to a quieter part of the beach to soak it all in.

Looking out over the sea, I leaned back on my elbows and dug my toes into the pale sand. This moment was much better than any alcohol. I took a deep breath and tilted my head back to feel the sun's warmth on my face. For a long while, I simply lay there, enjoying the sound of crashing waves and talkative sea birds.

A barely audible splash caught my attention, and I glanced toward the water. A large grey seal peeked its head out of the water a little ways off from shore. It turned its head from side to side, as if scoping out the beach. Almost like it was trying to find something...or someone? In all the times I'd seen seals, I had never witnessed that kind of behavior. This one appeared almost humanly intelligent. Its beady black eyes connected with mine in what felt like a challenge, and then it ducked under the water's surface.

I rose to my feet, unable to believe my eyes. Had I really just seen that? My wolf rumbled in my chest at the supposed challenge, but even he knew we stood no chance against a seal in the water. It would outswim or drown us. Wolves weren't known for their prowess in the sea. Besides, my mind might've exaggerated what had happened. The alcohol might still be lingering in my system; although I doubted it, since werewolves metabolized everything, from food to drugs, much faster than humans.

The only seal shifters I'd ever heard of were selkies, but they were mythical creatures, not real. Then again, that's exactly what humans thought of werewolves. What was I supposed to believe? I walked farther down the beach, closer to where the humans lingered, and kept my gaze on the water. If I could get another look at the seal, I might figure out what was going on. But the animal was gone.

I settled back onto the beach. The quiet peace I'd felt before had left me, only to be replaced by a strange curiosity. My wolf growled in agreement with me, for the first time in a while. Hope swelled in my chest, but I pushed it down. It was too soon to relax. Tension spread through my body and left my muscles feeling like cables pulled too tightly, ready to snap at a moment's notice. We would take things a day at a time. I couldn't help feeling a surge of relief at the apparent progress, though.

Going out tonight in wolf form to reconnect with my beast didn't seem as daunting anymore. Perhaps we were finally working through our issues, but I had to remain in control: no fighting with anyone, human or otherwise. Just remain calm, despite my beast and the nightmares. I blew out a steady breath as I slipped my shoes on for the return trip to my cottage.

As I turned to leave, I froze. The petite blonde from the pub sat on the beach, close to the footpath. She wrapped her arms around her knees and stared out at the water as if mesmerized by it. I'd have to pass her to be on my way.

Never before had I felt such hesitation with a lass. My beast, on the other hand, wanted to know her. The last full moon was half a week ago, so our reaction to her couldn't have been due to the moon's power. Maybe Mike was right. He'd pointed me to her. This could be fate, as well as a reason not to use alcohol as a crutch.

Could a lass cheer my sour mood? Silent warning bells unsettled me. What if I couldn't remain in control? What if I hurt her or accidentally revealed my true nature? No, I couldn't involve myself with her, regardless of the pull I felt.

She glanced in my direction and cocked her head to the side, reminding me of the seal earlier, then raised her hand in a wave.

Damn, she had to notice me.

6

UNNA

*W*hen I lay down for my nap, I just tossed and turned, unable to sleep. The water whispered sweet nothings, calling me back to her. My human legs were at times cumbersome, and traveling on them was much slower than swimming as a seal, but I smiled when I finally made it to the beach. Any pain in my feet left me as I stared out over the blue water and the beauty of the sea caught me in her grip. *Home.* Somewhere out there, my kin swam below the waves. A pang of loneliness struck me in the chest. While I didn't want to be with Ægir, I hated being homesick.

That's when I saw the red-haired man from the pub. He stood a little way off, closer to the water. A scowl scrunched up his angular features as he stared at me. Could it be the sun was in his eyes, or was it me? I blinked and waved, not sure what else to do. *Stay calm. Try to act human.*

He exuded an aura of danger, like maybe he wasn't exactly human either. I wasn't used to being on land, but he was different from the people I'd seen. He strode over to me after a few long moments, and his facial features melted into a neutral expression, even if he held himself rather stiffly.

"You're the lass who stared at me during lunch." His deep, masculine voice warmed my insides, catching me by surprise.

My eyes widened, and I scrambled to my feet. "Uh…yes. That would be me." I wanted to cover my face with my hands to hide the blush that rose in my cheeks. He really had noticed me watching him earlier. How embarrassing. I hadn't imagined when I snuck all those glances that I'd actually speak to him.

"You're not from around here." It wasn't exactly a question, but I nodded in response. "Are ye on holiday?" He shoved his hands into his pockets, probably against the February chill in the air. Cold weather didn't bother me much, even in human form. Granted, this was nothing compared to the temperatures farther north, closer to where my people spent most of their time. But I mirrored his actions and pretended to feel the cold.

"Yes, I'm here for a few days to enjoy the sights. Scotland is beautiful." I glanced back out at the sea. Any nervousness I felt at talking with him instantly dissipated. I let out a breath I hadn't known I was holding. Pleasure radiated from the top of my head to the tips of my toes at being in the sea's presence.

"Aye, I ken." He turned toward the water as well. "I'm Colin. What's your name?"

"Unna." He tilted his head to the side and raised an eyebrow at me in question. "It's a Faroese name."

"I see. That's a pretty name. I haven't had the pleasure of visiting there." The cool wind blew again, ruffling his red, curly hair. I watched the smooth strands softly wave in the breeze, and it took all my strength not to touch him. A soft splash made me shift my gaze back to the water. Before I could see the source, whatever had been out there was gone.

Colin's gaze followed my own, and we looked out there together.

"Lots of seal activity today."

"That's nice. I wish I could have seen them too." His words saddened me a little. My kin were out there beneath the waves. I wondered if some of father's warriors were out watching over me, or if they were truly seals. Whoever it was, they didn't let me get a look at them.

I stared back over at Colin. An odd attraction drew me to him. He wasn't like Murray, trying to force his friendship on me. He didn't show much emotion, but for some reason, I wondered if he did like me. There was something about the way he acted around me, and I had seen his glances at the pub too. I knew I wasn't the only one feeling this strange fascination.

"I'm sure if you stay long enough, you'll catch a glimpse of them." He bowed his head to me. "As much as I'd like to stay and chat, I need to head off now. Perhaps I'll see you around at the pub."

My heart leapt into my throat. I didn't want our time here to come to an end. "I'd like that." He started to turn away. "Uh...what about tomorrow around dinnertime?" I smiled at him, and he gave me a half-smile in return.

"I'll save a table for us. See you then." Without another word, he headed off along the path back to the road. I watched him go. He was a lot taller than me, and his clothes were snug enough to prove he had firm muscles tightly coiled beneath the surface of his skin. His feral aura excited me in a way I'd never felt before, and I was looking forward to dinner a lot more than I should have been.

The thought of sitting on the beach and watching the waves didn't soothe me as much now, especially if my father had his warriors out there spying on me. This was my time, my trip on land. But it comforted me that I was missed. At times, I'd wondered if my father was so overcome by his unrelenting grief that he didn't realize I was still here.

Colin paused on the trail just before it twisted around a hill that would take him out of sight. He looked back at me and waved. His eyes green eyes sparkled with gold flecks I hadn't noticed before, and then he was gone.

I raised my hand even though it was too late, then dropped it to my side. The only people on the beach now were a fair distance away, checking out the large cave with a guide.

With one more glance at the sea, I started off back to the cottage, steeling myself for the long walk. For some reason, it seemed to take longer going home than it had to get to the beach. Maybe because I'd had a more positive attitude when I set off than I did now. At least I had a meeting with Colin tomorrow to look forward to. I'd implied to Murray that I would call him, and that might be fine since he had a car, which would make it easier to see things farther away. But I didn't want to spend all my time with him, especially now.

Being with Colin at the beach had been refreshing. He hadn't been as scary up close as I'd thought he might be. My thoughts were so focused on our meeting at the beach that I blinked in surprise when I realized I was back at my kin's cottage. I opened the door and instantly felt myself relax a little. I enjoyed my time around humans, but hiding away here from the chaotic human world felt comfortable. Even though I loved exploring dry land, I needed space to be alone. I wasn't used to interacting much with others, especially not with my mother gone.

However, I couldn't escape from the pull of the ocean—the soft caress of the currents I'd always called home. I didn't think I ever would, especially not after I was mated.

Hunger weakened my knees, even though I'd eaten at lunch and only a couple hours had passed. My human form appeared to need food more often. It could've been all the walking, too. My feet were still sore. I made my way to the kitchen. Human cooking was out of my comfort zone, but Ailsa had left a large notebook with instructions on how to feed myself, and some other things of interest about the human world.

Even as I read through her handwritten notes, my mind returned to Colin: the sight of his red hair blowing in the breeze and the sparkle in his green eyes. My heart beat faster just thinking about him. I might not be adept at being human, but at least I'd secured more time with him. With a smile, I pushed thoughts of him away and focused on reading.

Some of the recipes in this book were complex enough to warrant their own notebooks, but others were simpler and more my speed. After a few moments of going back and forth between the easier ones, I set my mind on stovies and started gathering the ingredients.

One thing that struck me was that even though I'd tried to remain unnoticed, both Colin and Murray were interested in me. The scene in the pub replayed in my head as I chopped vegetables. Why had Murray been jealous of Colin and vice versa? The men had acted strangely, but I could barely understand the males of my own species, let alone those two. I definitely had more to learn.

But I was glad Murray had driven me here, even if he'd come across so pushy. Walking still felt a little weird. Having my legs support my entire weight was tiring. Ailsa had set out foot cream to help soothe them. The thick socks I wore were no match against the painful blisters that appeared. As I put the vegetables to boil, I wondered if Murray would be willing to drive me to town tomorrow. After all, he had seemed interested in spending more time together. Ailsa might ask questions, and I knew she relayed messages to my father's men for him. If she saw me with Colin, she'd probably tell my father that I was mingling with human men. I didn't want my time here cut short.

I put bite-sized chunks of beef into the pot with the potatoes and onion and stirred it. After I ate, I could figure out how to use the phone and call Murray. Trying to find a way to ask him to come over tomorrow occupied my thoughts so much that the timer on the stove startled me. The words would come to me when I called, I was sure of it.

The stovies smelled delicious. Pride welled in my chest at the sight of the meal I'd prepared. I set the table and inhaled deeply, savoring the aroma before taking a bite. The first thing I noticed was the warmth of the food, heating me against the coldness that crept into the cottage as the sun began to set. The second was the succulent flavors. It was like nothing I could find in the ocean.

Hesitant knocking drew my attention away from the last few bites of my meal. Was it normal for humans to drop by and visit one another? The village was small enough. Maybe it was appropriate here, but I had no memory of my mother ever mentioning uninvited visitors. The second set of knocks was louder and more confident.

I chewed on my lower lip and went to the door. To my surprise, it was Murray with a shy grin on his ruddy face. Without invitation, he took a step forward, invading my personal space. "I was worried when you didn't ring. I'm on my way back to the town to meet my pals, but your place was along the way. Just wanted to be sure you're okay out here, lass," he said, a sharp bite to his tone.

Humans rarely discussed things on their doorsteps, and since he was practically inside already, I stepped away from the door to let him in. "Actually, I was going to call you after dinner. I have something to ask you." I was almost done with dinner anyway. At least this saved me the trouble of figuring out the phone.

Murray walked past me straight into the living room. "Ah, I wasn't aware you were eating. I dinnae mean to disturb your supper. I've been on my feet all day. Mind if I sit?" He slumped onto the sofa without waiting for an answer.

"Sure. Don't worry. I was just cleaning up." I hurried over to the small kitchen table to put my dishes in the sink. From the corner of my eye, I saw Murray take in the interior of the cottage as he had after lunch. My heart raced, and I suddenly felt exposed with him here. I had to remind myself that I wasn't prey here. He was just a man who enjoyed my company. Right?

"You're staying in a lovely cottage. I don't think I've seen too many people out this way. Such a shame. I guess it's a good place to relax for a while, but there's no television here," he mused as his eyes locked with mine.

I nodded, not knowing what to say to that. Maybe it didn't have all the amenities humans were used to, but I enjoyed this place. The atmosphere in the cottage grew a little more tense here with Murray, but I couldn't risk suspicion. Let him think of me like those tourists on the beach. It was better than him learning the truth. I walked the few feet into the living room to join him. There wasn't much furniture here, so if I wanted to sit, I'd have to be right beside him on the couch.

Relax, Unna. Relax. I let out the small breath I'd been holding as I sat beside him. We'd been seated fairly close in the pub, but I hadn't thought much about it then. Perhaps my nerves were getting the best of me now. I had no reason to feel so uptight.

That's what I kept telling myself, at least.

"How long have you been in town? I'm not sure if I asked before. What sights, in particular, would you enjoy seeing?

My schedule is a little different than normal at the moment. I'm a fisherman by trade, and my poor boat is in the shop for repairs." My stomach did a flip at his words. He was a fisherman... "I don't have much to do right now. I'm working with another fishery out east for money to get it fixed." He propped his arm on the back of the sofa, all but looping it around my shoulders. While I knew humans had to provide for their families in whatever ways they could, some of my friends and extended family members had been caught up in fishermen's nets and killed. And my mother...

Nausea punched me in the gut, and I sprinted to the bathroom, mindless of my painful blisters. I couldn't remain with Murray any longer. I collapsed to my knees in front of the toilet. Tears streamed down my face as the contents of my stomach were forced up in waves.

Heavy footsteps sounded in the short hallway, and I glanced over to see Murray frowning down at me from the doorway. "Are you okay? I hope you didn't get food poisoning." He grabbed a towel from beside the sink and wet it under the faucet, then handed it to me. "You don't have anyone else around here to take care of you, do you?" Softness warmed his eyes, and he looked once more like the kind man I'd first seen in the restaurant.

I shook my head and wiped my face and mouth. My knees trembled when I tried to stand, and he wrapped his arm around my waist to keep me from falling. I flushed away the mess in the toilet bowl, then washed my hands and splashed cool water on my face. "Not really, no." There was Ailsa...but I doubted she'd understand. "I have no one else here. Just me."

Before I knew what Murray was doing, he swept me off my feet and carried me to my bedroom on the other side of the hall. I blinked up at him, startled, but he set me gently on the bed and covered me with the soft blankets.

"Rest now, lass. Do you think you'll be okay, or shall I stay with you?" He looked a little tired. I couldn't expect him to stay here. Not after all he'd done for me already.

"I'll be fine. Thank you. I'm sure it's just an upset stomach." My eyelids grew heavy, and sleep pulled at me like a waning tide. I blinked up at him, pretty sure I'd missed something he'd said.

"Good girl. Rest now." He kissed my forehead, and I had a fleeting awareness of his retreating footsteps before I drifted to sleep.

7

COLIN

With darkness ruling the sky, I couldn't wait much longer. The beast within me stretched toward the surface of my skin, growing ever more impatient. I'd kept him on a short leash so far. This would be our first hunt in these seaside hills. The cottage showed the signs of my misery: a few empty bottles and a general unkempt look. Enough was enough. I couldn't backslide with my wolf. We needed to fully reconcile before we suffered the consequences.

I slid out of my clothes and draped them over the back of a kitchen chair, plotting the course of our run in my mind. Open fields would allow us to freely sprint, and a small wooded area would yield prey for us to hunt. With night settling in, I didn't have to worry about the neighbors noticing anything. There weren't many around, and the ones who were would likely be tipsy at this point in the day.

Outside, I put my key under the welcome mat. The owner hadn't even had the door locked when I'd arrived. No one worried much about burglaries around these parts.

Insects chirped and birds flew overhead. Prey would be on the run. With a smile, I knelt in the lush green grass and let the change slide over me. My body welcomed the wolf, returning to the shape as if it was what we were supposed to be. My bones broke and tendons snapped, only to reshape themselves in my wolf's form. Claws protruded from my fingertips even as the digits shrunk into large paws. I looked up at the waning moon, and a soulful howl poured from my throat.

For the first time in a while, my wolf hadn't fought for control during the shift. He was just happy to walk in his own form again after the past week. Tales had echoed through my head of those who lost control to their wolves. They spoke of being trapped inside one's body, unable to fight their wolf's desire to roam the countryside killing whatever crossed their path.

My wolf sent a sharp nudge my way, urging me to move as he grew more and more impatient. If I didn't do something soon, I feared I'd have to fight for control again. My wolf couldn't view me as a submissive being. We needed to come to an understanding and build trust again.

I took a few hesitant first steps and felt the ground beneath my paws come alive. Spruce needles on the ground gently touched the padding on my feet, mixing with the moist sensation of grass underneath. I had missed the feeling, the scent of the evening air. What began as slow steps became a jog, then an outright run as joy spread through my chest.

My wolf let out a soft yip of pleasure as we sprinted through a glen. The more we ran, the more unity I felt. But we lacked the one thing that could truly bring us together again—a hunt. I took my senses back, and we stopped for a few moments to drink from a small stream running through the glen. A squirrel chattered at us in alarm and ran up a tree.

My sister would've climbed up and had it for an appetizer, but sadly wolves weren't the best climbers.

We pushed onward to the edge of a well-kept field full of potatoes. The scent of rabbits was all over the field, but we had our mind set on something bigger. My neighbors, an older farmer and his wife, were nowhere to be seen on their dark farm. Perhaps they were at the pub having supper. Their old dog was asleep on their porch.

We took a detour around the property. I wasn't worried about the dog or farmers, but I didn't want them to stumble upon us and get hurt. The area around the house smelled heavily of the dog and their two cats. Nothing seemed out of the ordinary. Next I walked over to the old hen house. The scent of a red fox was all over this area, but the farmer had done well in placing the fence. The fox hadn't found a way inside. The chickens were quiet and asleep. A grin played upon our lips as we thought about the fox. Usually our smaller cousins stayed away from areas where we wolves roamed. Apparently, this one was hungry enough to venture into my temporary territory. With a huff, we headed toward the wooded area.

As soon as we hit the tree line, we found exactly what we were looking for—deer. The musky scent, marking all the nearby trees, reassured both of us that the deer we hunted was male.

We approached more slowly now, listening as we tracked it deeper into the woods. It wasn't long before we caught its scent. It was close. Staying downwind, we edged toward a small clearing in the forest and saw our prey grazing. It was alone, and more than large enough to satisfy our ravenous hunger. My wolf grinned, flashing his sharp fangs. Now the hunt was on. Soon we'd be feasting.

Just as I stepped closer, two things happened: the wind shifted, and a branch snapped beneath my massive paw. The buck lifted its head. *Oh, bloody hell.* We dashed toward it, keeping to the shadows in the hopes that it wouldn't see us, but it caught our scent. Its eyes widened and it turned to run. Within moments, it was headed straight for the dense brush behind it, but we had outwitted smarter prey than this before. The sound of its wild escape was audible even over the thundering beat of our heart as we plowed through the trees after it, digging our paws into the dry forest floor for better traction. This was our favorite part, the moments we both loved. It would all be over soon.

We caught sight of the deer again and threw everything we had into the chase, using the last reserves of speed we'd kept back for this moment. It tried to kick us, but we were at its side now, not behind it. The deer started to change directions, but we leapt through the air, latching our massive jaws onto its throat. The deer's musky scent and the coppery taste of its blood filled our nose and throat. It slowed and tried to shake its head, but dropped to the ground. We jerked our fangs back, ripping out its throat and giving it a quick death before eating.

The meat from our kill went down bite after hungry bite. The struggle for power between me and my wolf had lessened as our fragile bond tightened once more, a tentative first step to becoming whole again. At least the threat of losing myself to my beast wasn't as great anymore.

Cleaning myself didn't take long after my wolf's instincts kicked in. I didn't want to return to the cottage covered in gore, but I'd be taking a shower before hitting the bed anyway. I moved away from the kill to rest under a spruce tree. The rest of the carcass would be taken care of by the other animals in the forest. The mossy ground acted as a bed while I let my meal digest. A series of excited yips soon erupted from the forest behind me. Apparently the fox had kits, and they'd all found the deer.

My wolf snarled a little at the disturbance, but I quieted it down. We'd enjoyed our share. The deer belonged to the forest. Maybe this would keep the fox fed for a while so it wouldn't try to sneak into the hen houses.

I stood and loped back toward the cottage. With the kits bouncing around, I wouldn't be able to nap. Besides, I craved a hot shower. After that, I'd clean up the place and finally get my shite together.

8

UNNA

I dreamed vividly for the first time in ages, of my mother laughing with a younger me on the beach. The brilliant twinkle in her eyes when she smiled was like nothing I would probably ever see again. Being away from her hurt my heart. I missed her so much. Her life had brought so much happiness and light to our pod, but most importantly to our family. While my father had suffered more deeply from her loss than I had, I still carried a secret hope that she was still out there and that I might see her alive someday. However, if she was, she'd likely have found her way back to us one way or the other by now. She was resourceful, and a lot more human-savvy than most selkies, so for her to have been carried away by a human fisherman made me concerned about my own chances. But I hadn't done anything to make anyone wonder about my heritage. I was just a girl on vacation from the Faroe Islands. Aside from Murray paying a little too much attention to me, I didn't feel like I had anything to worry about.

When I stepped out into the cottage's main living area, I noticed all the dishes had been washed and everything was put in its place. It looked just as it had when I'd left for the beach. My eyebrows rose in surprise. It was sweet of Murray to have done all this for me. I'd planned on cleaning up before I did some further exploring, but he'd saved me time to have fun and do more of what I wanted on land. My first stop today would be visiting the caves near the beach. I'd wanted to see them up close for a while now, but I'd never dared venture closer in my seal form. Someone observant might realize I wasn't a normal seal. Besides, regular seals didn't hang out much in this area, due to it being frequented by a decent-sized pod of selkies.

My father had never allowed me to come too close to shore after my mother went missing. He was afraid of the same thing happening to me, but I hadn't thought that would come to pass. Sometimes I wondered if he just worried too much, but I knew not to push fate. I didn't want to repeat the past and hurt him more.

A sharp knock on the door made me jump and bump into the kitchen table. I turned toward the front door, careful to check out the window first. A familiar-looking truck sat in the driveway. Murray.

Did I say something to encourage him to come back here today? I didn't remember anything like that. I bit my lower lip, wondering if I should even answer. If I didn't, he might think I was out exploring Durness. But that would be wrong, particularly after he'd been kind to me last night and then cleaned up the dishes on top of it. I didn't want to ruin that kindness with my own suspicion.

I plastered a smile on my face as I opened the door, even if I wasn't feeling particularly happy to see him. "Hello there, Murray." I stood in the doorway. Just because I was acting polite didn't mean I wanted him to come inside. My plans for the day were made. I wanted to head out and have an adventure. My unexpected guest wouldn't ruin that.

"Hi, Unna. It's good to see you looking more healthy and lively. Have you eaten yet today? I could show you around more like I mentioned last night." He took a step closer, but his eyes narrowed a little at me when I didn't move.

I didn't have any recollection of agreeing to him coming by today. My heart dropped into the pit of my stomach as I remembered him saying something I'd missed when I was on the brink of sleep. I grimaced, unable to hold back my annoyance.

How stupid of me. I'd been so tired I hadn't been aware of what I'd agreed to. Now I was stuck with hanging out with him today. He was all right, but I didn't enjoy spending time with him like I had with Colin. Murray enjoyed hearing himself speak and getting his way. But it didn't sit well with me to rebuff him. I'd just been hoping to explore the land, without feeling as if I was being watched the whole day. I didn't have that problem when I was among my own kind. Most of the time we enjoyed a relaxed atmosphere, where we could be together but not be on top of one another.

"Oh, I'm sorry. I guess I was tired last night. I didn't pay as much attention to what I was saying as I should have." Frowning, I ducked my head and looked at him through my eyelashes. Part of me wished he'd just leave.

Murray stared back at me. The good-natured smile I'd come to expect from him slipped from his lips. Disappointment crept into his gaze, and I kicked myself for speaking to him like that. "Aye, you were tired, lass." He glanced over my shoulder as if expecting to find someone else there with me. "Guess I'll be on my way then." Grunting, he turned to leave.

I blinked, my shoulders slumping forward at the hurt evident in the way he held himself. "I'd be happy to fix you that tea we missed last night at least." The words slipped from my lips before I could hold them in. I wanted to be on my way, but the least I could do was offer him the courteous gesture of tea. My mother had mentioned that humans were as keen on manners as we were, if not more so.

He stopped almost in mid-step, then slowly turned back to me. For a moment, he glared at me warily, but the look melted away and morphed into one of hopefulness. "If you're sure about this, lass. I don't want to be bothersome to you."

My eyebrows drew together at the comment, but I moved away from the door to let him in. "I'm sure. I haven't eaten breakfast yet, but I have some smoked salmon and bread to start my day. You're welcome to some as well."

"That's fine. Just tea for me." He closed the door behind him as he stepped inside.

I walked into the kitchen to put water on to boil, then set about getting the cleaned cups from last night and two tea bags. When I checked on him again, he was standing in the short hallway, staring into my bedroom. His gaze was fixed on the chest where my sealskin was stored. My heart raced, and I clenched my hands into fists. *Stop freaking out.* He was harmless. What would he possibly do? He couldn't know about selkies. But…he *was* a fisherman.

"You're quiet," I said. "Is everything okay?" I forced a smile back onto my face when he glanced in my direction.

"I'm fine." He took a few more steps toward the bedroom and the chest before turning to face me. "That is a lovely chest. Can I see inside? The craftsmanship is like nothing I've seen for quite some time." A curious glint flared in his eyes. He watched me carefully as if cataloguing my reactions. Why had I agreed to let him stay? If he didn't leave, I wasn't sure what would happen next. Would I be dragged off like my mother?

"I don't think that's a good idea. The chest is pretty old, and I don't have the key. Besides, it's not mine. I'm just staying here. I wouldn't want anything to happen to it." Most of that was true, but I did carry the key in my pants pocket. If he looked inside the chest, he'd see my sealskin and he'd know. He'd be able to use my otherworldliness against me. If he wanted to, he could take me as his bride, so long as he had the pelt in his possession.

"I see." He returned to the living room in silence. Something in his demeanor had changed. He sat on the couch and stared off into space, which only heightened my agitation.

I brought the tea over. My hands shook a little as I set the cups on the coffee table. We remained there together for a while—him sipping his tea as I ate the smoked salmon as an open-faced sandwich. The delicious food rejuvenated me. I couldn't believe how hungry I was, likely as a result of getting sick last night. I was still a bit embarrassed about that, but it was over. I hoped it wouldn't happen again.

The morning snack went on in quiet of my kin's cottage. The atmosphere was much different than it had been yesterday. He wasn't talking my ear off or trying to get super close to me. His arm wasn't wrapped around my shoulders. Perhaps he'd gotten the hint, but something in his gaze made me think differently. The longer he was here, the more often he glanced in the direction of the bedroom. Did he know something was up?

"It's about time for me to get cleaned up. I should be heading off soon." I almost said where I was going, but cut myself off at the last moment. He might decide to show up at the pub or try to convince me that I should ride into town with him. Meeting Colin was exciting, and I didn't want Murray to mess that up for me.

Murray didn't say anything. He grabbed me by the hips as I reached for the tea cups, then flung me onto the sofa. I beat my fists against his chest, but any power I had as a seal was locked into my pelt. This human form was weak. Before I could figure out what he was after, he began shoving his rough hands into my pockets. When he didn't find anything in the front, he flipped me to my stomach and dug into my back pockets, finally coming up with the key. Panic clawed at my throat. I rolled back over, punching, kicking, and screaming—anything to help my cause. But I knew it wouldn't do me any good. The cottage was out in the middle of nowhere, a ways off from town so we could come and go in seal form or nude as we needed, without attracting attention.

He climbed to his feet, but I rose up with him, struggling to snatch the key back. He slapped me across the face, the force of the blow knocking me back into the sofa. My teeth rattled a little in my skull, and I tasted blood. I placed a hand to my cheek and stared at him with wide eyes. His normally red face was bright pink with effort. "Dinnae mess with me, lass, or you'll be hurt worse." His threats scared me, but I couldn't let him win this. If he took my pelt... My stomach hurt just thinking about it.

I screamed at him, wordless and almost animalistic, then leapt from the couch and threw all my weight into him. He didn't budge, just pushed me back like a bothersome gnat. I didn't have any way to defend against him. He was big and male, and I was a slender human female who had skipped a few too many meals in my travels to reach land. But I had one thing he didn't—a fiery persistence to not end up stolen away like my mother.

I hopped on his back and wrapped my arms around his throat as he barreled through the small cottage toward the bedroom, and ultimately the chest. Every instinct within me said to keep throwing myself at him until he gave up, or until one of us was dead. He couldn't steal my pelt. If he did, I'd be his captive bride. Maybe I'd be better off dead.

I'd been promised to become the wife of one of my

father's selkie warriors. Father's patience was already short with me after I'd insisted on coming above the waves. If I didn't return, would he think I'd planned this? No, I doubted that, but I'd be proving him right and leaving him that much more heartbroken. I hated to think what he might do. Would he hurt himself? He'd tried to show strength for me and my siblings from his second wife, but I didn't want to think about what this kind of loss might do to him.

Murray knelt and jammed the key into the lock, apparently not taking my attempts to hurt him very seriously. He didn't even seem that uncomfortable with my arms around his throat, but then again, he was a big man. I slammed my right fist into the back of his head as the padlock opened. He swung around with me on his back, and my hold slipped before I could re-secure my grip. I flew off and crashed to the floor, my head barely missing the nightstand. He lifted his foot as if to kick me, but something almost tender flashed through his eyes. With slow, controlled breaths, he lowered his leg to the ground. "Lay there until I say you can get up." The cold violence in his words froze me in place. I'd already felt the pain of his touch. From the look in his eyes, I knew he could do much worse.

That didn't leave me with many options. Fighting wouldn't help anything. I could either submit to his will or flee back to the ocean. He would take my pelt if I got away, but I might be able to get help if there were other selkies around. I knew they didn't come very close to shore, though. With my pelt taken, my chances of swimming out to them would be slim. But what other option did I have? Bringing Ailsa into this wouldn't be safe, since she was human too. She wouldn't be able to fight Murray any more than I could.

Murray crouched in front of the chest, taking his time opening it as if it were carved from the most delicate of materials. Something told me he'd known what it was when he first saw it. Why hadn't I closed the bedroom door? I bit my lower lip hard.

"Don't, please. I... Don't do that." I slowly climbed to my feet as he pulled the sealskin from the chest, looking confused. Maybe I'd been wrong? Maybe he didn't know...

"What the bloody hell is this thing?" He glared at me, then back at it. And just like that, realization dawned in his eyes. He refolded it and laid it back in the chest. "That is a sealskin. Why does it mean so much to you?"

I opened and closed my mouth, trying to figure out what to say. I didn't want him to know what I was, but it was pretty obvious he was beginning to figure it out. So I kept silent, deciding to not say anything at all.

"You're a selkie, aren't you? The Faroe Islands are known for their selkie lore. It's not exactly logical, but it would explain why you have this here and are so set on keeping it secret." An arrogant smirk spread across his lips, and I wanted nothing more than to punch him in the face. "If I remember correctly, now that I have your pelt in my control, I can force you to be my wife."

My lips parted in fear, and I could only nod. My worst nightmare was coming true.

Nodding, he locked the skin back inside the chest and shoved the key into his pocket, looking a little more at ease. "My family always said I was destined for failure when it came to relationships. Now I'll finally prove them wrong." He patted the pocket that held the key. "If we're going to get married, I have some planning to do. The ceremony needs to be great to prove my good-for-nothing relatives wrong." He chuckled as he stalked forward, reaching out to grab me, but I jumped out of reach.

"Please don't do this to me, Murray." I stepped back again, putting my hands up in the hopes he'd stop this nonsense. "I have a life...a family." The words slipped from my mouth, and I immediately regretted them. Why had I said that? Now he knew there were more of us out here.

But he didn't stop.

I ducked beneath his arm and ran down the tiny hallway. The sound of his heavy footsteps spurred me on, despite my aching legs. I threw open the door and sprinted across the large field, heading for the water. It didn't matter if I drowned in the sea. I needed to be away from him and back to where my family could find me. At least then my father would have some closure, the kind he'd never gotten after my mother's disappearance.

His harsh breathing and stomping steps behind me drove me to run that much faster. I refused to look back at him. There was no way I'd let myself be caught. I powered on, my legs springing me over the ground quicker than I could have imagined. Maybe being human wasn't as mundane as I'd thought. Murray's footsteps grew ever closer, but from his labored breathing, I could tell the chase was wearing him down. If I just kept pushing on…

"You're supposed to be my slave. Aren't you afraid of me destroying your precious sealskin? I could tell everyone I know about you and your kind." His voice faded into the distance as I kept running from him.

But I didn't answer. It would break me to lose my sealskin. I wondered if I'd die, but then I couldn't see living as his wife either. I couldn't…not after the way he'd attacked me. He was a monster.

"Suit yourself." His footsteps stopped altogether. "You'll come back to me. I'll be waiting for you when you finally come to your senses. We'll be happy together. You'll see, lass."

My heart thundered in my chest, not only from the running. Fear pulsed through my veins, and I snuck a glance over my shoulder to see him with his hands on his knees trying to catch his breath. His eyes were fixed straight on me.

I gulped and took off toward the coast where I'd first come on land.

Once I was sure he wasn't still following me, I slowed down to a brisk walk. The sound of crashing waves filled my ears. My heart hurt looking at the vast waters, knowing my pelt was locked away under someone else's control. Even though I'd run, I knew I was nothing more than a slave to Murray. He was right. It would only be a matter of time before I crawled back to him. It was woven into my people's magic. He had a right to marry me regardless of how I felt about it. My soul filled with dread and a desire to walk into the waves until the air left my lungs.

Sobs wracked my body, and I fell to my knees in the water, then slumped onto my side. I slid my hand through the cool waves, feeling an ounce of peace fill me, but it was like a candle's flame in a vast pit of darkness.

The waves were quiet. There were no selkies around. I was alone in the world, and I only had myself to blame for getting into this mess. If I hadn't come on land in one last bid for freedom, I wouldn't be trapped in an impending marriage to Murray.

I hadn't liked the idea of being with Ægir, but it would've been a lot better than being tied down to a violent human whose emotions seemed to change on a whim.

9

COLIN

*L*ast night's hunt had soothed my worries and brought me that much closer to my wolf. *Things might just be looking up for us.* I grinned. Getting back in touch with the wilderness might be exactly what I needed. Lord only knows I hadn't breathed in any fresh air when I was locked in the research facility. The salty seaside air was even better than I remembered. This was one of the things I'd missed about my home country. But while I enjoyed being back, the events that happened upon my return to Scotland had hurt more than helped my road to recovery. Both the wolf and I were barely hanging on, and taking it out on one another as a result. If I wasn't careful, my beast might slip my tenuous grasp, and I could be lost forever.

Caitlyn couldn't know how far I'd fallen in my control. I still kicked myself for leaving without saying goodbye to her, but I hadn't known when she'd wake up, and if Dougal had realized the poor shape I was in, he might not have let me leave. Learning the truth about what kind of man my father was, and what he'd done to my sister, had just about sent me over the edge. Anger boiled in my veins at the thought. My jaw clenched tight, and I balled my hands into fists at my sides. *Och!* If I didn't stop this, it would escalate into something much worse. Any progress I'd made last night with my wolf would be for naught. No, I refused to go down that path.

The scent of seawater and sand carried to my nostrils. Yesterday's excursion to the shore had also helped bring me peace. Something about the sound of waves crashing against the shore took a weight off my shoulders. Maybe I'd even find Unna here, though I had plans to meet her later for dinner. The path toward the beach was off to my right, but I opted to sit on a cliff overlooking the sea instead.

I scanned the waters. Part of me hoped to see the seal from yesterday. Had I imagined the sharp intelligence in its eyes? Now that I knew what I was looking for, maybe I'd be able to tell.

I let out a breath and started to lean back on my elbows when sobs echoed up from the beach, startling me out of the serene moment. I froze. The more I listened, the more familiar the voice sounded. Curiosity rose up within me. There were only two people that I knew out here: one was Mike, the bartender, and the other was Unna. This voice was definitely female. My stomach clenched. Had something happened to her? No one should have to suffer through horrors without any help, like my sister had.

I stood and walked toward the edge of the cliff. Below me on the beach, a blonde woman lay on her side in the sand, sliding her hand through the water. My heart froze in my chest. Unna. I was almost sure of it.

The way her hand lovingly caressed the water and the heart-wrenching sorrow of her sobs made me wonder about her intentions, being so close to the water. I couldn't just stand by while she hurt that way. If she took her life... I had to see if there was anything I could do.

I hopped down from the twenty-foot cliff, landing silently in the sand. She didn't move from her position, so I doubted she'd heard me. "Unna? What's wrong?"

She staggered to her feet and spun around to face me. Her pale face was red and puffy from crying, and her wide eyes widened further when she saw me. Recognition glinted in them, and she took a couple steps back, soaking her bare feet in the cool water.

"Are ye okay?" I repeated, my brogue thickening as emotion warmed my chest.

She bit her lower lip and stared at the sand below us. Her mouth opened, but she didn't say anything at first, as if she didn't know how to answer the question. Finally, she shook her head. "No, I'm not really." She let out a long sigh.

"What's the matter?" I took a step closer, but she didn't move away this time.

"I...I don't know if I should tell you. Things have gotten out of hand since I've been here. I only wanted an escape from who I am. I...I'm not what I seem to be." Tears dripped from her blue eyes as she met my gaze. "But I know there's something different about you too." She gave me a once-over. "I felt it when you first entered the pub yesterday."

I straightened my spine, feeling ready to bolt, but I took a deep breath. While she mostly smelled human, there was a foreign scent about her, something watery that I'd missed before, almost like a seal. My mind wanted to reach for the obvious. The seal from yesterday who had been too humanly intelligent, thoughts of selkies...but no, that was mad. "What are ye?" I raised an eyebrow at her.

Her shoulders slumped forward, and she choked on a sob. "I don't know who to trust, but something about you feels right." She dropped to her arse on the sand, and I knelt at her side. "I'm terrified. My people... I'm not from land." Her big blue eyes stared up at me as if begging me to believe her. "I'm a selkie."

Amazement flowed through me, and I stared at her, not sure what to say. While werewolves were seen as magical and mysterious to humans, in the supernatural community, we were relatively common. I'd never heard of real-life selkies walking around on land before. They were mere myths. I was from Scotland. It stood to reason if something like that existed I would've known about it, particularly since the Scottish Pack had been around here for ages. No one had ever mentioned it.

"You don't believe me," she said, her voice breaking with pain and frustration.

"No, it's not that." *Lies.* But I did trust my nose. My nose pointed to a sea creature...to a seal, which made sense with what she told me. "I do believe you. I just never thought your kind were real." I sat beside her, keeping a comfortable distance between us. Her pale blonde hair flowed over her shoulders and down her torso. I wanted to run my fingers through that silky length as I stared into her eyes, which were blue like the sea itself. "What's wrong?"

She dipped her toes into the water, and I wanted to pull her away from there. She'd freeze her feet if she kept that up. The water was cold this time of year. While selkies might not deal with things like hypothermia in the water, I was pretty sure she could still freeze her human limbs. She drew away from the water and looked over at me. "My sealskin was stolen."

I wracked my brain, trying to remember what little selkie folklore I'd heard. I couldn't be sure that what humans knew was the whole truth. Humans thought they knew a lot about werewolves, but most of what Hollywood portrayed was slipped to writers in the olden days to throw humans off from the truth. If they believed all sorts of strange things, they'd have less power over us. It worked, for the most part.

"Your pelt is how you get back to the ocean, isn't it?" I followed her gaze to the crashing waves.

She nodded. "Who I am is in my sealskin. This isn't my natural form. It's the part people readily accept when I come on land, but..." Her voice broke again. "I don't think I can survive without my skin. I need the ocean. It calls to me."

I could understand. If the part that allowed me to turn into a wolf was taken, I wouldn't know how to cope with its loss. Especially not when I'd grown so accustomed to that side.

"Who stole it?" I could give a good guess, seeing as how she'd left the pub with Murray, the man who couldn't keep his hands to himself. If he knew what she was, then it seemed like just the kind of thing a guy like that would do. I was coming to learn there were lowlifes wherever I went. Maybe I should have gone somewhere without any people at all. But then I wouldn't have met her. Anger surged through me like a tidal wave at the way Unna had been treated. My bones ached as my beast rose to the surface, ready to change and take revenge before I could have any say in it. But that wouldn't accomplish anything other than upsetting Unna more than she already was.

From the look on her face, I could tell she'd sensed my inner turmoil as my beast tried to take control. She shivered and scooted away from me.

"Who...what are you?" she asked. The fear in her voice faded, replaced with awe. "You're very different."

I grimaced. I hadn't wanted to expose myself to anyone. Even if I helped her, I needed to keep my identity safe, because I didn't really know her. If she told anyone about what I was, if she used it to get back her pelt or anything like that, then I would find myself in a terrible situation. I shook my head. "It's not a good idea to tell you." On the other hand, she'd displayed a lot of trust telling me who she was. Perhaps I was too hard on her... Time would tell.

She opened her mouth to argue, but the sound of footsteps nearby in the soft sand made me glare at her to remain quiet. Her already pale skin whitened that much more, and she looked over to see an elderly couple walking along the beach hand in hand. Sighing, Unna bunched up her knees to rest her chin on them. She looked so young and innocent. The pose reminded me of Caitlyn, sitting in the Pack's cage as the memories of what my father did to her came pouring back in.

My temper flared just thinking about my father, but I schooled my face, keeping a pleasant demeanor and speaking a few polite words to the elderly couple as they passed. My beast fought hard to gain the upper hand, but I squelched him. Unna scooted away a little bit farther, as if she could feel my inner struggle. However, we both knew if I went after her, she wouldn't be able to escape.

"Who took your skin?" I asked again once the couple was out of earshot.

"Murray." She cleared her throat a little. "The man I had lunch with at the pub. You saw him." She returned her gaze to the sea. The longing in her eyes scared me. If she walked into the waves, I could pull her out, but with the depth of emotions radiating from her, it might be a struggle to keep her away.

"I see. When was the last time you saw him?" I brushed a lock of hair from her face as it slid down like a silky curtain.

She shivered a little at my touch, but she didn't move away. "Not long ago. He chased after me when I fled my kin's cottage, but he told me he'd be waiting when I came back. I don't plan on doing that. My mother was taken away from me when I was younger. I won't be a victim like she was." Her gaze pinned me in place with its conviction. "I'd rather die."

10

UNNA

I looked up at him, surprised he'd touched me. His skin was so warm it bordered on hot. The thought of curling up beside him as he wrapped his arm around my shoulders invaded my mind, but I forced that idea away. While there were decent humans like the elderly couple who'd just passed by, this man—whatever he was—was not human, and maybe not altogether friendly, even though he seemed to care about my situation.

The glare he'd given me had made my heart skip a beat with its ferocity, and for a moment, I could see something predatory pass just beneath his face, as if there was something else living inside his skin with him. The idea both frightened and intrigued me at the same time. Maybe we were similar. Could I have met someone else who understood my plight?

He pulled his hand away as if burned by the touch of my skin. "Where is your kin's cottage?" He looked toward the cliffs and the small passage I'd come down from. "How did you know he wouldn't find you here?"

"I didn't. I just had to be closer to the sea. Part of me

hoped I might find another selkie here to help me, but then I found you." I looked up at him through lowered lashes. Maybe this was all meant to be.

He shifted his position as if nervous at the prospect of me considering him my protector. While he did intimidate me, there was a sense of honor to him, even if I suspected he failed to admit it to himself. He was certainly a lot braver and more of a man than Murray and his friends ever would be.

"I assume you were keeping it there and he took it from where you're staying?" He leaned back onto his elbows. His T-shirt clung to his hard abs, and I marveled at his physique. The male selkie warriors of my people were handsome and quite seductive to human women, but something about this man enthralled me.

I jerked my gaze away from him. "Yes, he did. I'm afraid to go back. If he's still there, he might think I'm agreeing to become his. If he marries me, I'll be stuck as his obedient wife unless I can reclaim my pelt." I felt more than saw Colin move closer. He brushed his hand over my arm, and heat sizzled within my body in ways I'd never felt before.

"Dinnae worry. I'll make sure you're not subjected to that."

"Thank you. You surprise me. I don't know who you are or what you are, yet you give so selflessly of yourself to help a selkie you didn't know existed." I smiled despite myself. Even though he was sort of standoffish, he was kind. He would protect me against Murray and hopefully make sure I wasn't locked into a relationship with him against my will. That gentleness lit a fire in my chest. Tossing myself into the waves didn't seem necessary anymore. Perhaps Colin had only seen ordinary seals yesterday—the selkies didn't come near shore much around here—but I had found someone who would help me.

"You're welcome, Unna." His hand lingered on my skin

before he leaned back in the sand again, and we watched the waves. "You're not actually from the Faroe Islands, are ye?" He smiled at me. It didn't brighten his dark green eyes, but his grin still stole my breath away.

I shook my head. "No, not really. Unna is my human name, though. My mother gave it to me before we visited there together a long time ago." I balled my hands into fists in my lap. "She was taken by a fisherman after we'd been on shore for a couple days. I haven't seen her since." Pain tightened the corners of his eyes and the smile melted from his lips. I instantly regretted telling him about my hardships. Somehow I knew he was dealing with an equally biting pain, and I'd enjoyed his smile too much for it to just disappear like that.

"Nothing is going to happen to ye, ye ken? I'll make sure of it." His Scottish brogue grew thicker with each syllable until I could barely understand him, but he spoke with such passion that I nodded, wanting to believe every word.

"Thank you." I wasn't one to physically connect with others. My kind loved one another, but touching wasn't a typical part of our relationships, aside from those few special bonds such as my father and mother had. But emotions welled within me, and I threw my arms around Colin and hugged him.

11

COLIN

*T*he sudden hug sent me off-balance, and I ended up flat on my back with a selkie woman laying across my chest. I put my hands on her back at first, unsure what else to do. It wasn't every day that someone initiated physical contact with me, and something within me burned at the feeling of her this close. She called to a hidden piece of me, as if there was a deeper meaning to my attraction to her. Even my wolf craved the closeness with her, and I knew he wasn't focusing only on sexual desire. But this didn't make sense. Unna and I were nothing alike. She wasn't a werewolf—she didn't even live on land. When her time was done here, she'd go back to the sparkling depths of the sea to be with her family and all the other selkies. There would be no way for me to stop her. It wouldn't be my right. If I let my feelings get the best of me, she would break my heart, and possibly her own.

While I wanted to help her, I needed to keep her at arm's length. I'd be better able to save us both from ourselves that way. Besides, she'd just opened up to me about how her mother had been taken away. If I fell in love with her, I'd be doing the exact same thing. I'd be no better than the man who stole her pelt. The only difference between him and me would be the heartache I'd feel after losing her to the sea.

Which was a perfectly good reason to not let myself be entranced by her beauty. I hugged her back for just a moment, feeling the boniness of her ribs and her small pert breasts against my chest, then nudged her to the side. I didn't want to end the contact between us, and my wolf snarled at me below the surface of my skin at doing so. He couldn't understand that I had to do what was best for both of us.

"*Dinnae fash yersel.* It'll be fine." I stood, brushing sand from the back of my jeans. "Since your place isn't the safest, I think ye should come to where I'm staying until we can get your pelt back and handle the man who stole it from ye." I offered her my hand to help her up.

I could handle the man who had stolen her pelt on my own, but this encounter had put me off-balance. I wasn't at my best right now. If I let loose and ripped into him, my humanity would be history, and I'd be serving the humans knowledge of my kind on a silver platter. They'd know we weren't beasts of myths and folklore, and I'd already gone through the consequences of that first hand, in the United States.

The idea of returning there when I came back to my senses didn't particularly appeal to me. What if danger still lurked behind each rock or tree? Threats were still possible in Scotland, but I felt even less safe in the country where I'd gone through the horror of being locked away and treated like some lab rat.

Shuddering, I snapped back to my senses as Unna placed her hand in mine. The coolness of her touch lit a warmth in me that I didn't think was possible. I lifted her to her feet effortlessly. The cottage where I stayed was a decent hike, and she wasn't wearing any shoes. I didn't want her feet to get hurt on the trip there. "Let me give ye a lift, lass." Her hand was still in mine, and I reluctantly let go. What was coming over me? This was bloody insane. Not at all the reason why I was in Durness, let alone good for me when my emotions were already so volatile.

"What do you mean?" She looked toward the path that led to the road.

"You can ride on my back. It'll be more comfortable than walking on your bare feet." I shrugged a shoulder. "My place isn't exactly nearby, so it'll be quite a hike." I tried to sound only like a concerned friend, but the idea of her being pressed against my back excited my wolf.

She just smiled at me as if my intentions were pure. "Okay, if you insist. I've…never done something like this before." She walked behind me and stood there, waiting.

I knelt a little. "Put your hands on my shoulders, then hop up and wrap your legs around my waist." She did as I instructed, but as she wrapped her legs, she kicked me in the stomach harder than a human female would have. Air burst from my lungs, and I groaned, leaning over a little but staying upright enough to not drop her.

Unna froze behind me as if she'd done something terribly wrong. "Are you okay? Did I hurt you?" Her small hands pushed at my shoulders, but I clutched her calves firmly to keep her in place.

I focused on slowly drawing the air back into my lungs so I could talk again. "I'm fine," I gasped at last. "Just caught me off-guard. Sorry to have startled ye."

"I'm sorry as well. I didn't mean to kick you." She reluctantly placed her hands back on my shoulders and settled in as I straightened my spine.

We'd already stayed here long enough. I didn't want to scare her by running too fast, but we needed to get out of here quickly. So far I hadn't sensed any humans other than the older couple, and two teenagers farther along the coast making out, but I had no idea if Murray would come to the beach after her.

My attention span around Unna made it impossible to catch all threats coming our way. If I lost sight of our surroundings, we'd be asking for trouble.

"*Dinnae* worry. I'm sturdy. I can handle it." The run back to the cottage was freeing. Unna yelped at the speed and tucked her face into the crook of my neck. Her hot breath enticed me, sending shivers along my spine. More than a few times I wanted to lay her on the ground and ravish her, but I shook those thoughts aside.

Stop. Fucking stop. I couldn't let myself get attached. That would be the worst possible thing for us. I had to remind myself that she would be going back to the ocean. Plus, I had a responsibility to make sure my sister was safe, and then I'd be going back to the United States to re-join my new Pack.

"Are you all right?" she asked, leaning in close again.

I glanced over at my left shoulder to see her face a hairsbreadth from my own, watching me. I sighed, wondering what exactly I should say. Should I be truthful or just deny it all? It would be better to distance myself. I couldn't unleash my emotions on her. That wouldn't solve anything for either of us. Instead of answering, I ran faster, unable to help my grin as she squeaked in response.

Within ten minutes, we'd made it back to the cottage. Sweat slicked my torso, making my shirt damp, and I knelt enough for her to slide down my body to the ground. The feeling of her soft breasts pressed against me had made the run that much harder. I needed a cold shower, for more than one reason.

"Here ye go. Make yourself at home." I unlocked the door and let her walk in before me. Drawing in a deep breath, I scanned our surroundings to make sure no one had been snooping around outside while I was gone. I'd had no problems in my time here, but having Unna with me made me that much more paranoid. To my relief, the only scents around were ours and that of a nosy rabbit that was long gone by now.

For now, we could relax. But I knew someone as well-connected as Murray would probably do whatever he could to get Unna back for his own purposes. I just needed to make sure we stole back her pelt and got her to safety before that could happen.

"Thank you. You have no idea what this means to me." She turned around after walking a few feet into the cottage, to look at me with genuine appreciation in her eyes.

"Aye, I do. For now, just keep the door locked. I'm going to ask around to see if I can get any information on Murray. If we can find where he lives, we might know where to go to steal your pelt back." I brushed a strand of her pale blonde hair aside and smiled at her. "Don't let anyone in while I'm gone."

Her eyes widened, but she nodded. "I won't. Promise you'll be safe."

"Aye, I promise." With that, I turned on my heel and left for the pub. If anyone had any useful information around here, I was betting it'd be Mike.

COLIN

urray. I should've known. If only I'd listened to what Mike had tried to tell me, but I'd been stubborn. Unna had paid the price for that, too. Part of me wanted to end him, another just wanted to see him suffer. Neither option would be beneficial to us, especially since I didn't know where he was. From what Unna said, he'd come by her place whenever it suited him. A soft growl built up in my throat as her words ran through my head again.

Murray would keep the pelt somewhere close to himself, somewhere he knew was secure. I hadn't been around the village long enough to learn all the gossip, so I had to place my bet on the person who usually knew best—the bartender. The village was small enough that it was likely Murray and his friends frequented the pub daily. The thief and his band of rowdy jerks had certainly known their way around the bar.

I picked up my pace as adrenaline burned through me. The agitation I felt drew my wolf closer to the surface than I wanted. *Calm yourself before it's too late.* With some effort, I took a few deep breaths before breaking out into a steady sprint. Pretty soon I'd be coming up on the town, and I'd be a danger to everyone if I shifted now. Besides, I needed information, and it'd be difficult to talk in wolf form. I grinned at the thought of what everyone's reaction in the pub would be, though.

My uneventful run finally ended, and I paused in front of the pub's parking lot. The place was more unpopulated than I'd seen it before, but it was far from empty. However, I had a good chance of catching Mike's attention. The air outside of the pub was the same as before: filled with the smell of ale, food, and the garbage in the alley to the side of the building. Murray's scent wasn't in the air, which was for the best. If I saw him now, my wolf would likely take over and rip out his throat.

A handful of older Scots were seated at a table toward the back of the pub, talking quietly to one another as I entered. They seemed to be the only other customers, but then again, it was after the lunchtime rush. Mike let out a sigh and raised his hand in a wave. "I almost thought you wouldn't come, lad. A shame that you're back to the drink. Many have gone down the path yer starting on, and fewer have come back from it," he said, reaching for a pint glass. It sounded like he spoke from experience.

Shaking my head, I sat on the barstool closest to him. "Nae, I'm not here for that. I came to talk." His grey eyebrows shot up towards his receding hairline. I frowned at him, not sure I liked his surprise. "Remember the lovely lass from last night? She and Murray had an…altercation. I want to find him so we can sort out a few things, ye ken?" I leaned closer to him, though I doubted the older men in the corner could hear me.

To my surprise, Mike chuckled and shook his head. "Aye.

I told you to reach out to the lass. You should've listened, lad. You might've saved her from all this trouble. What did Murray do to the girl?"

Stole her pelt, left her in fear for her freedom, and tried to trap her into a loveless marriage. I cleared my throat and tried to keep the anger pulsing through me from showing on my face. "I don't know if it'd be appropriate to repeat without the lass's permission. Where might he be around this time of the day? Does he work? A local address? Anything?" My voice came out calm and neutral, even though I wasn't feeling either of those things.

Mike scratched his chin, looking torn between his customer's privacy and helping Unna. "Hmm… He blathers on while he's drunk, but I might need a few moments to recall what he's said." He nodded toward the menu in front of me. "Why don't you get something while I have a think?"

Seriously? Was there anything more cliché than that? With a grumble, I glanced through the menu and ordered two shepherd's pies, one for here and one to go. I wasn't sure when the last time Unna had eaten, but I didn't have much in my cottage for her. Besides, I didn't feel the siren's call to alcohol as I did before. Knowing Unna was counting on me motivated me to raise my personal standards. Also, if Mike decided not to help me out, it would only be a matter of time before Murray or one of his friends came wandering into here.

The pub didn't take long to serve my order, but while it was authentic, it was heavily salted. Apparently the kitchen liked their customers thirsty. When I was nearly halfway through the meal, Mike leaned against the bar in front of me. "You know, I do remember something. He was a nice, quiet lad when I first laid my eyes on him. A fisherman just like his father and grandfather, going back a few generations. All quick to anger and slow to cool. Hard headed, sorry lot that dinnae know when to quit." I raised an eyebrow at him. The genealogy lesson could wait until after he gave something more concrete. "Tsk. You're quite impatient, lad. Anyway, the man's boat is in for repairs by the docks. The last time his little crew was drinking, they commiserated about needing to work out toward the east, helping out a fishery there. He needs the money as he's not too adept at managing his expenses. Apparently he's better at drinking than savin' his coin for hard days. But you didn't hear that from me." He winked.

Mike talked for another ten minutes, giving some more information on Murray and his family, recounting some of the sob stories he'd heard. The last few years had been hard for Murray. Not only had his boat been damaged multiple times by his handling of it in the rough waters, but his drunken friends had caused a small fire on it, nearly costing him his license to operate. He was single, had trouble following anyone else's orders which made employment hard, and had a family that nagged him about marrying. That last part explained why he was so adamant about being with Unna. The only things in his possession were an old house and his boat, neither of which were said to be too appealing.

That, at least, gave me a starting point. Murray would likely keep the pelt in one of those places. He could possibly have left it at Unna's cottage as well, but that didn't seem as likely. His boat and home were both personal to him. After all, he probably spent as much time on his boat as he did at home, if not more. Mike gave me rough directions to his house and pointed me toward the docks. It wasn't much, but I could use my nose to help guide me there.

As I rose to leave with the extra shepherd's pie in hand, one of Murray's friends walked into the pub. I drew the man's scent into my nose, memorizing it so I could track him if I needed to. He smelled of fish and oil, betraying that he'd been working on a boat recently. If he was here, Murray and the rest might arrive soon enough.

13

UNNA

*C*olin had been kinder to me than I'd expected. I wasn't sure how I'd ever repay him for the fact that he'd helped me, and now let me stay with him. I stood near the door for a few minutes after he left, not sure what else to do. Being in his home without him here unnerved me a little. It was larger than my kin's cottage. I had to keep reminding myself that I was safe here.

Colin kept the place a little unkempt, so I picked it up, putting things in order and cleaning as best I could from my memory of Ailsa's manual. The kitchen had a strong aroma of chemicals, and I bit my lower lip wondering what had happened in there to require so much cleaning. All the tidying up didn't help, because the more time I spent away from my pelt, the more worried I became. Was it still in one piece? Would I be able to tell if he destroyed it? Maybe I should've accepted my fate and gone back to Murray. I tried to be strong, to push aside the fear that he might destroy it in his anger. If he did, I would never be able to return to the water. I'd be stuck on land and torn away from my family forever. What would happen to my father if he lost me too? Would he ever know what happened to me?

I looked at the phone sitting beside the couch. My pod's caretaker Ailsa might be able to get a message to him, but I couldn't remember her phone number. I'd stared at the numbers, trying to memorize them in case I needed them, but now with all the emotions bubbling up inside me, my mind went blank. I tried to center myself and calm down, but I couldn't. I didn't want to end up like my mother, kept away from my people in a loveless relationship.

Tears slid down my cheeks, and I brushed them away with the back of my hand. My mother's smile was what I remembered the most. If I needed any proof that she loved me, it was in that sweet gesture.

I dropped onto the couch and wrapped a flannel blanket around me, suddenly cold. When I started the day I had so many high hopes for it, but now as I glanced outside at the sun beginning to set, I felt hopeless. The one thing I had going for me was Colin, but would I be putting him in harm's way? I didn't want to drag him into this, but I had no other options. The moment I rested my head on the sofa's arm, my eyelids drooped, likely from the exertion of running away from Murray earlier. But I didn't want to sleep with Colin gone. For some reason, I felt safer with him.

My body relaxed into sleep regardless. Dreams of the sea welcomed me with open arms. Life was peaceful beneath the waves. Fish and all sorts of sea animals swam by me. Out of nowhere, a heavy rumbling sounded above me. I tilted my head back curiously and swam toward the sound.

Farther below me, I heard other selkies calling my name, warning me to stay with them, but I didn't pay any attention to their cries. The closer I came to the surface, the better I could see what the intrusion was. A fishing boat. My heart leapt into my throat, and I spun around to flee from it.

Shouts from the vessel sounded above me, and a loud splash pierced the waves a moment before pain radiated through my side.

Roaring, my father swam toward me, but the spear the fishermen had thrown into my side was dragging me toward the boat.

I squirmed to try to free myself, but it only made things worse. The spear was too deep, and blood seeped from my torso, staining the water around me red. My eyes drifted shut as I was hoisted out of the water. A loud banging caught my attention, and I looked up at the boat to see Colin there. He reached out his hand for me while the fishermen fought him. My gaze dropped back down to see Ægir and my father in the water, also holding out their arms for me. I knew Æegir wanted me to bear his seal pups and to inherit my father's place as leader of our pod when Father gave it up, but I didn't want that kind of utilitarian relationship. I desired so much more than that.

The thumping continued, and I jerked upright on the couch. Sweat covered my body, causing my baggy shirt to stick to me.

Who was there? Colin had keys to his home, and I highly doubted he'd be knocking so forcibly.

Murray.

My heart pounded in my chest. Fear drew its long cool finger up my spine, causing me to shiver. Should I answer? If I didn't, maybe he'd just go away. The banging suddenly stopped, and I wondered if whoever had been there had left, but that didn't make sense. I tiptoed to the door. If it was Colin, he could be injured, or worried that I wasn't answering. The window on the door had a curtain, and I drew it a little to the side.

I froze at the sight of the selkie male on Colin's doorstep. It'd been a while since I'd last seen Ægir in any form, especially as a human. He was the mate I didn't exactly want, but he was strong and capable of reigning over the pod when my father's time was at an end. I just didn't want to be tied down to him. My calling was beyond our pod, and I wondered for the first time if it might be with Colin. I desperately wanted to go back to the sea, but I couldn't help thinking that Colin was kind and strong—things I wanted in a relationship.

The concerned look on Ægir's face worried me. Had something happened to my father? I opened the door, instantly kicking myself because Colin had asked me not to let anyone in. But I couldn't shut Ægir out. I had to know what unsettled him, even if I didn't want to hear it. But what if Colin arrived back now? I had no idea how long I'd slept. If the two of them met, I had a feeling the results would be explosive. Ægir needed to leave as soon as possible.

Also, something wasn't right with Colin, and I really wanted to help him. He seemed too on edge for his own good. The problem with Murray was still outstanding, and I needed him to be more in control than he had been before. If he lost it in public and showed the darkness hiding within him, he would be putting everyone at risk.

"What's the matter, Ægir?" I asked, lifting my chin, trying to project more strength than I felt.

He bowed his head toward me. His pelt circled his waist to cover his nudity, but I kept my gaze on his face. "What are you doing in this home? You should be back at our cottage, not here. Your father gave you explicit instructions." A frown curved his lips. "Where is your pelt? I don't sense it nearby."

I opened my mouth to reply, but the words died on my lips. How could I tell him that it was taken from me? I couldn't go back to our people's cottage, not with Murray buzzing about there. He'd swoop in and grab me, forcing me to become his wife before I could build up the strength to protest again. I'd have to be his wife, unless I was lucky and he left the key to the chest around. I had a feeling he was too smart for that.

Ægir grabbed me by the arms and gently shook me, refocusing my attention on him. "Speak to me. I know you don't wish to be my bride, but I am of your people. Don't shut me out in your time of need."

I raised my gaze to meet his and closed my mouth. Without speaking, I took a step back to let him in. He couldn't stay long, but I didn't want to have this conversation with him outside. He should know what happened, if anything to tell my father that I wouldn't be home for a while. At least then he'd have closure, and I wouldn't be missing like my mother, a forever floating question mark.

14

COLIN

I leaned against the building, remaining in the shadows as I watched for Murray. I wanted to get to him before he went inside, that way I'd be able to *talk* with him before he met up with his friends and gained strength in numbers. Not that I was concerned about them beating me, but the less anyone knew about me and my goal to get back Unna's pelt, the better.

Murray was possessive, and he already had a grudge against me from Unna gazing at me when we first met. The feeling was definitely mutual. The thought of taking care of him once and for all crossed my mind, and my beast growled in agreement. But I couldn't do that. Not here, not yet. My beast and I were still too weak from the science facility to hold ourselves under control. I didn't want the beast to take over for good.

That was a little more likely to happen than not given how things were going, but something about being with Unna also strengthened me beyond what I could've expected. Being with her and knowing her, and maybe even wanting her, drew me back to my human self, healing the ravening beast that lay beneath my skin. Even my wolf wanted more of her, and he was willing to support me to gain her favor.

My thoughts consumed me so much I nearly missed the truck that pulled into the parking lot. Its headlights drew near to where I stood, and I slid further into the shadows. A familiar man hopped out and looked around. *Murray.*

I stood up straighter, wanting nothing more than to punch the bastard in the mouth. His shoulders were tight, and the look on his craggy face was grim. He appeared to be on the lookout for someone, probably Unna. How stupid did he think she was? She was at my home, safe and sound. I wanted to get this done and head back to her as soon as I could.

I couldn't imagine the pain she was going through being without her pelt. That pain would soon pass. I'd promised to help her get it back, and I would. I wanted her here with me, even if I knew that wasn't what was best for her. She had a life under the waves, one I wouldn't keep her from. As a werewolf, I knew how painful it was to be kept outside of my element.

Memories flooded me of the white, sterile room, always smelling of bleach and other chemicals. The bars held me captive like some kind of wild animal.

The crunch of feet on gravel threw me out of the flashback.

Murray walked toward the pub's entrance. I darted toward him to catch him before he went inside. His hand reached for the door, and I grabbed him by the shoulder, pulling him away from it. He was a stocky man, so it took more than my human strength to get him to the side of the building with me, especially with him flailing his arms. While he was a big guy, he apparently didn't know how to fight.

My Pack mates sparred with one another often, both to increase our skill if we ever needed to deal with humans in a mundane way, or if we were ever going up against another werewolf. It was a matter of survival. We couldn't always be in wolf form.

"What the shite? Oh, you...the girlie's little boy-toy." Murray spit the words at me, and I pushed him against the building, hard. He gasped for breath, then shoved away from the wall, heading for the front of the pub to get to his friends. I wasn't about to let that happen.

I grabbed him again and shoved him against the stone building, this time keeping my hand on his shoulder to hold him in place. "Where you going, arsehole? Nowhere fast, is where. If ye have any self-preservation, you'll answer my questions. Where's her pelt?"

Murray narrowed his eyes at me and tried to move, but I kept him in place without much of an effort. My wolf growled, and I bit the sound back to keep it from bubbling out of my lips. We didn't need him to know we were supernatural. The Scottish Pack wouldn't be happy with me if I went around exposing us, and the last thing I needed right now was trouble with them, especially with Duncan in charge. I only hoped he was taking good care of my sister. She deserved a much better brother than me.

"Pelt? I dinnae know what you're talking about, boy." His words were rushed, and I could smell the slight fear that betrayed his lie. "If you don't let me go, you'll regret it. There aren't a lot of rentals in town, and I reckon I can find out where you're staying and make life hell for you."

My wolf snarled, furious that he was threatening us. This time I didn't hold back the sound. I let him know exactly how I felt about what he had to say. "It's goin' to be that way, then?" I cocked back my fist with every intention of punching him, but I couldn't guarantee that I wouldn't flatten his face and kill him. My beast was so close to the surface that I was nearly shaking with the effort to stay under control.

"Murray, what's going on, mate?" a man said to our left.

I glanced over to see his friends staring at us. They didn't have any visible weapons, but I wouldn't want to get into it with all of them. If I killed anyone, my beast would snap, and I feared for everyone—innocent and otherwise—if that happened.

I released Murray and patted him on the shoulder. He visibly winced, and I wondered just how hard I'd been squeezing. "Nothing. Have a good evening."

"Wait a minute. You're the shite-bag who kept us from nicking that liquor from the bartender." The shortest of the bunch, the rowdy one, stepped forward.

Murray held up a hand. "Just go inside and order me a stiff drink. I'll be there soon, I promise, laddies." He turned back to me when they left. "I don't know what your intentions with Unna are, but she's mine. Don't think you can whisk her away like some treasure thief." He shoved against me, and I stumbled back a couple steps, surprised that he'd think I was trying to steal her away instead of honestly helping her. Was that what she thought as well? Did she think I just wanted her as a wife, to serve me and provide children for me?

I watched as Murray walked off, and stood there scratching the little bit of stubble on my chin. I knew where he might be keeping the pelt, but now I needed to find out when he wouldn't be around so I could go snooping. More than ever, I needed to be near Unna, to convince myself that I wasn't like him. I wouldn't keep her chained to me against her will. She was free to be who she was.

I grabbed the takeaway bag with Unna's food from the roof of a nearby car and stared at the pub's door. *Fucking shite.* I didn't need any more reasons to worry.

15

UNNA

The longer Colin was gone, the more I worried about him. Murray might be out searching for me, and he still had my pelt, which I desperately wanted back. My soul might die without it, though my heart cared for Colin. Life would be empty without my pelt, and I wasn't sure if I'd even have the strength to continue living. I might find that out soon if we didn't retrieve it.

Ægir continued to stare at me, and I twisted on the couch to look at the wall instead of him. He shouldn't even be here. Colin had told me not to let anyone in, but I'd needed to hear Ægir out. Besides, I did want to send a message to my father, since I'm sure he was probably worried about me. I was supposed to be spending only a few days at the cottage, and my time was coming to a close.

"I… My sealskin…" The words wouldn't come, even though I tried to spit them out. It was something no selkie ever wanted to say. "It was taken." The sentence tumbled from my lips, and I clenched my hands into fists in my lap. "I need you to tell my father what happened. He can't be left to wonder about me. It would kill him."

"You don't have to stay here." He swept his hand around at the cottage. "Come with me. We'll reclaim your pelt together. You will be back in the sea with me and your father again in no time, not stuck here on land with these humans." The quirk of his lips was arrogant, and he placed a hand on my shoulder.

It took everything in me not to flinch away. I opened my mouth to correct him, but stopped myself. Colin wasn't human. He was beyond them. I couldn't be sure what he was, and I couldn't help the mix of fear and attraction I felt for him. But he wasn't the one who did this, and he shouldn't be blamed for me being in this situation. "No, I can't leave." If I wasn't here when he got back, he might lose it and think I'd either run away or that Murray had taken me. Nothing could be done until my pelt was found, anyway. I wouldn't be able to see my father, because he never came on land, especially after my mother was taken.

Ægir grabbed my wrist and pulled me to him. As a warrior of our people, he was much stronger than me even in human form, but I couldn't let him take me. "You're coming with me. I know you're compelled to remain here, but it's not in your best interest. I can help you get away."

"No! I don't need your help, and I'm not compelled." I slapped my palms against his bare chest, trying to free myself, but he only tightened his grip on me.

"You might not realize it, but you really do, Unna." He threw me over his shoulder, and I yelped in surprise at the way he was handling me. He had never been one to touch, and now he was putting his hands all over me, forcing me to go with him against my will.

The doorknob rattled a little as someone put their key in the lock. *Colin.* My heart pounded in my chest, and I flailed my arms, kicking and punching Ægir with all my strength. He finally set me on my feet, but he placed himself in front of me as if I needed the protection. "Just stay behind me and keep quiet," he murmured.

The door opened to reveal Colin sniffing the air the way an animal might. He looked confused and frowned at us. "What's going on here?" He dropped a plastic bag on the small table beside him that smelled of delicious food.

My heart ached at his kindness. I had to explain what was going on. I tried to dart around Ægir to go to him, but Ægir held me back. I rammed my shoulder into his side to get him off me, but this time he clenched my wrist almost to the point of pain, holding me in place.

"Thief. You can't have this one. She's a daughter of the sea." Ægir's voice boomed with his command. "Bring back her pelt immediately, and I won't have to hurt you." He took a foreboding step toward Colin, dragging me along with him.

"Who is this, Unna? Why is he here?" Colin looked between me and Ægir, anger reddening his ruddy complexion. "I told you not to let anyone in."

"He's a selkie too. He thinks you stole my pelt and won't let me explain the truth."

"Hush, Unna. Let me handle this." Ægir shoved me behind him again even as I struggled to get to Colin's side. I couldn't believe I trusted him more than Ægir, one of my own people, but I did.

Colin clenched his jaw, and he lunged at Ægir. Before I knew what had happened, Colin had one of his hands around Ægir's throat. With his other hand, he pulled me to his side. "Don't even think about stepping between us. I don't know or trust you. You're apparently not paying attention to anything Unna says either, so that tells me you're not here to help her."

Ægir reached for Colin to try and fight him off, but he was obviously outgunned. He swung his leg up to kick Colin in the side, but the impact hardly seemed to make a difference to Colin. He just stood there like a statue, intimidating and more than a little scary.

I backed away from the men, but I knew I couldn't hide. Colin looked like he wanted to kill Ægir, and if he did, that would be on my conscience. I had to stop this, even if I was a little bit afraid to get between them. What if they went after me too? I was, after all, the reason they were fighting.

"Stop, Colin. Please." My voice shook a little, and I took a step toward him. I ran my hand over his arm, feeling it tremble with effort beneath my palm. I glanced at Ægir, and he subtly shook his head as if warning me away. He'd definitely bitten off more than he could chew with Colin.

"He needs to know his place," Colin said, lifting Ægir up so his feet no longer touched the ground. Neither man was small in stature, but Colin definitely had the edge in strength. I was pretty sure he could've thrown Ægir without much effort if he wanted to.

Ægir made a few muffled gagging sounds, like he was trying to speak. His face became more and more red, and I knew if I didn't do something soon Colin might kill him.

"Stop it! Right now, Colin...or..." He glanced my way, and I noticed his eyes had changed colors. They had been green before, but now they were wolf amber. "Or I'm leaving." He kept staring, as though nothing was really sinking in. "I'll go back to Murray." The words flew out of my mouth before I could contain them. I didn't want to do that, but it seemed like nothing else was getting through to him.

Colin threw Ægir to the couch, and the male selkie bounced off it onto the floor. Ægir placed his hand to his throat and cleared it a few times.

"*Dinnae* even think of insulting me like that, Unna." Colin shoved past me toward the door, then turned to glare down at me. "I'll not have that. If you want to go with him, then be my guest. Be gone by the time I'm home." He slammed the door behind him, and I jumped at the loud bang.

I couldn't believe he was gone. What had I done? I ran to the door to chase after him and explain I'd been stupid for saying that, but he was nowhere to be seen. I fell to my knees in the grass and looked up at the stars. The only person who cared enough to help me was now gone, and I'd royally messed it up. I had nowhere to go.

Ægir placed his hand on my shoulder and knelt beside me. "You don't want to be with someone like that. I'd never hurt you." He gently took my chin in his hand and turned my head to face him. "Come back with me?" He was acting so friendly now, but I knew this was for show. Soon he would expect offspring and a position of strength among our people. I didn't blame him for it. I just didn't want to be a part of a loveless pairing.

I wanted the kind of relationship my father and mother had, not a match of convenience. I shook my head. "I'm sorry. I can't do that. I need to be here. My pelt is still missing. I can't return to our people."

"Let me help you find it." He tried to pull me closer to him, but I kept him at arm's length.

I looked around the lightly wooded landscape outside Colin's cottage. He would be back sooner or later. I needed to make it right with him, if for no other reason than my gratitude for how much he'd already helped me. I couldn't let him think poorly of me. "No, I'll find it myself. Return to our people and deliver my message. I'll try to be back by the end of the week." I pulled away from Ægir and walked back inside.

"You can't possibly think to stay here. That man was more like a beast than a human. You'd be in danger. And what about what he said? He doesn't want you here." Ægir placed his hand on my elbow, pulling me back toward him, but I jerked out of his grasp.

"You don't know anything about him. I hurt him, and I need to make things right. You're not human enough to know about stuff like that." I spat the words at him, but I stopped myself from saying anything more. I was angry with myself, but I didn't need to take it out on Ægir. He wasn't the enemy. My loose temper would only make things worse for myself if we did end up mating. I needed to go inside, calm down, and wait for Colin to come back so I could make him understand just how sorry I was.

16

COLIN

I watched from the woods, hoping she'd stay but knowing she had more family out there who cared about her. I hated what she'd said to me, but I couldn't believe she'd actually go back to Murray, the horrible man who had tried to make her his captive bride. How could she return to him instead of staying with me?

I'd thought having her around and helping her assisted with healing my wolf's bond, but maybe the situation was hurting more than it helped. At least my control seemed somewhat better. I didn't exactly want to kill everything that moved. I counted myself lucky for not killing the male selkie.

Ægir spoke with her in hushed tones. I couldn't quite make out their words, but I breathed a sigh of relief as she shook him off and marched back inside my cottage. If she hadn't opened the door for him to begin with, this night might've gone a different way, but I couldn't fault her for wanting to interact with one of her people. She was stuck without her pelt, and we could only hope she'd get it back in time. What would happen to her if Murray destroyed it?

Would she perish? I didn't want to think about that right now.

I'd been able to dig up some information about Murray, but I doubted either of us knew whether the pelt was still whole or not. If I'd been able to talk with Unna, I could've asked her. I had to believe that it was. Unna would most likely have felt its destruction, wouldn't she?

The male selkie shook his head as Unna shut the door behind her, and then he walked back in the direction of the ocean shore. I rolled my neck and tried to relax in the knowledge that she'd stayed, even though I didn't exactly understand why she did. Ægir appeared more aggravated that she'd stayed than worried about her life. I wondered if he was why she'd been so interested in coming on land instead of settling down with a selkie husband. It made sense if she didn't feel wanted there. But I hadn't really talked with her about the subject—I was the last person to talk about relationships with. I was still upset with my own sister for being with my former Alpha. I doubted my sister knew what she was getting into, though. This situation was entirely different.

I turned away from the cottage. I wasn't ready to face her after our argument. I'd come too close to losing my temper, and I didn't want to accidentally hurt her. If she hadn't jolted me out of my rage, I very well could've strangled the selkie or broken his neck. Either way, it was best I take time to calm down.

I jogged through the wooded area back toward the farm where I'd snooped around. There wasn't much out in that direction, and I knew Unna was safe at my place for the time being. Even if Murray did come after her and try to find her, it would take time for him to figure out where we were. Besides, he didn't know she was here with me. For that matter, he didn't know my name or anything about me...

unless Mike gave away my information too. I'd like to believe he wouldn't do such a thing—I'd interrupted Murray's friends from helping themselves to his whisky in his pub, after all. A nice guy who didn't like the way those men behaved would side with me. But there was always the chance he might change his mind. He lived in the same town as them, and would have to continue to deal with them after I went on my way...

No, I was being paranoid.

Still, the thought disconcerted me. People made strange decisions under pressure, and while I could leave town and head away from here, the bartender didn't have that luxury. His home and business were here. Plus, I couldn't just leave Unna to fend for herself. She wasn't predatory like me. She was innocent. The thought of turning around and going back to apologize occurred to me again, but I couldn't see how that would be a good idea. Not after how things had been left. Maybe we both needed time alone to unwind before we got back into it. My beast was more restless than he'd been in a while, and I worried he'd hurt her, even though I knew he cared for her too, in his own way.

I rolled my neck again to push aside some of the stress bearing down on my shoulders, and found a spot under the open sky to lay and gaze up into the night. The soothing air calmed my beast, giving me a little bit more of myself back. I still remembered sleeping out under the stars a few times with my childhood mates, mostly in our wolf forms, and we loved it. Now I was mostly a loner. Even the new Southeastern Pack I'd been with hadn't noticed I was gone for quite a while.

17

UNNA

*T*he food Colin had brought was lukewarm by the time I ate it. It only made me feel worse about myself that I'd been so mean.

I placed my head on the couch's arm and waited...and waited. Surely he would be back anytime now? I was in his home. Where would he sleep? There weren't many other places to go, and I hated thinking of him out there when Murray could be looking for one or both of us. My stomach roiled, and nausea sat heavily on me. Not knowing how long Colin would be gone nearly killed me, but I did understand that what I'd said had been totally out of line. He probably needed some time to cool off, and I didn't blame him. I should've been the one to go off instead of him, but I had nowhere to go even if I wanted to.

If I wanted to live a life of suffering and sorrow, I could go back to Murray and be his slave-bride, but the last thing I wanted was to repeat what had happened to my mother. I had wanted the pleasure of visiting the human world before being mated off to Ægir, but all of my plans had gone awry. Now I faced exactly that future. The only one who could stand in the way of that was Colin, and I'd pissed him off. He had to come back eventually, but the waiting made me uneasy.

I placed my hands over my belly and stared up at the ceiling, listening to the night creatures outside. Everything was relatively quiet. Would it stay that way? This might've been a peaceful night if I hadn't screwed it all up. I shook my head, trying not to think about Colin. He'd come back when he was ready.

It felt like hours passed as I tossed from side to side, unable to find a comfortable position on the couch. I got up a few times, thinking I'd heard him, but it was just the wind or a small animal. Finally, when the sun was starting to light up the sky, I became too tired to keep my eyes open any longer and drifted off to sleep.

When I awoke, the sun was shining in through the window, blinding me. I shielded my eyes with the back of my hand, then squeezed them shut again anyway. I still felt sick to my stomach over last night's incident with Colin and Ægir. Here it was morning time, and the cottage was still silent. My heart sank. He wasn't home yet. What if he'd been injured while he was out last night?

This was all my fault. If only I'd kept my mouth shut about Murray and told Ægir to leave, none of this would be happening. We might be out finding my pelt so I could return to the ocean, where I'd be reunited with my father and bound by my duty to provide an heir to our selkie pod. I sighed and rolled over to face the couch. Heaviness pressed against my chest, and I didn't even want to get up now.

"You're awake." Colin's warm, deep voice startled me. I jerked onto my back, no longer caring about the blinding beam of sunlight. He was here, and safe. "I see you didn't leave, even after what I said." He walked into my field of vision and crossed his arms over his chest. He had a stern look on his face, and I wondered what he was going to do.

I didn't want him to be upset that I'd stayed. Would he be? From the look in his eyes, I wasn't sure, but I stood slowly, as if approaching a wild animal. "Colin, I'm so sorry about last night. I really shouldn't have said what I did. I don't want you to think that I really wanted to go back to Murray. I'm much happier here with you than with him. I was just... scared. Ægir is a jerk, but he's not the enemy. I didn't want you to hurt him, but that doesn't excuse my behavior."

I didn't put my hand out to touch him, even though I really wanted to. Just feeling his skin against mine might've made me feel less like I'd completely screwed things up between us. But I was scared. My heart raced in my chest, and I saw a flash of anger in his eyes before it was squelched.

He uncrossed his arms. "I know you didn't mean it. I saw how Murray treated you and how you were after being with him. He's not right for you. He just wants you as his slave. You're better off back in the ocean than being with Murray." He pulled me to him. He smelled like fresh-cut grass, and there was a blade of it in his hair. Where exactly had he gone last night? Had he slept outside?

I buried my face in his chest and frowned. My words were muffled as I said, "I know. Although, I'd be happier with you than with either of those options." I bit my lower lip hard, unable to believe the words that had come out of my mouth, but surprisingly—or not—they were true. He made me feel more than I'd ever felt before, even if some of that was fear. "You make me feel alive."

He stayed silent for a while, and I wondered if I'd said the wrong thing. Should have kept quiet about how I felt? Ugh...

After a while, he bent his head and breathed into my hair. "I feel the same way about you, Unna. I do." He sighed and pulled away from me. "Before we think about this anymore, we need to find your pelt. Then we can talk about all of our emotions. While I do care about you, it's better that way.

"Scotland will always be my home, but it's not where I live at the moment. If you want to have any hope of being near your family, then I'm not the guy you should be getting involved with." He turned away from me and strode toward the back of the house where his bedroom and bathroom were. I hadn't been back there much since I didn't want to intrude on his private space the way Murray had mine back at the selkie cabin.

I frowned at his back as he walked away from me, not sure what he was trying to say. I didn't want anyone else but him, and we were in his cottage. Where did he live if this wasn't his home? Was it far away?

"But I do want to know more about you. I don't wish to wait until it's all too late. What if you decide you don't want me then? I'd be all alone here. What if Murray were to destroy my pelt? I'd be stuck on land. Then where would we be?" I dropped onto the couch as the thoughts zipped through my head, making me feel sick to my stomach. If I was stuck on land without my pelt and without Colin, then I wouldn't want to live at all. If Murray were my only existence, then I'd go back to the ocean one way or the other.

Colin stopped, but he didn't turn around to face me. "I..." He cleared his throat. "I can't be your foundation. I'm not perfectly stable at the moment on my own." His voice cracked a little. I knew he was going through some things— anyone could see that from the way he acted sometimes—but I was going through a lot as well. I was being cast off on a journey without any compass.

Maybe I'd been wrong about Colin. Right now it seemed like maybe I was better off on my own. I looked away from him to stare toward the door of his cottage. I should just get out of here. He didn't want me around, and he was probably only helping me out because of pity or something. I had no idea why, but that wasn't what I needed or wanted. My disappointment that I'd begun to trust him hurt more than his rejection. I'd been so stupid to sit here in his cottage and wait for him like some defenseless child.

He strode off into the bedroom at last, leaving me all alone in the living room. I could hear him rummaging around, but I didn't care what he was doing. Perhaps it was my time to leave.

I didn't need this. I rose from my spot on the couch and went to the door. I opened it quietly, stepped outside, and turned to close it, to find Colin staring down at me. I gasped and stepped back. My foot slipped on the stair, and I flailed my arms as I lost my balance.

Colin grabbed my arm and pulled me into his body to steady me. "Where do you think you're going?" His terse voice had a hint of a growl to it, and his eyes shone a fiery wolf amber. "I thought you said that you didn't want to run off, and now you're doing exactly that? I'm not sure if I can—"

"No." My voice was nearly a shout. "Don't even think you can come down on me and use what I said last night against me. You basically want to cast me aside as if I'm nothing to you. Don't try to tell me you're broken and aren't a good fit for me. You don't get to tell me that. I can make that decision for myself. Unless you're just trying to get rid of me because you don't reciprocate my feelings."

I tried to push him away, but it was like wrestling with a brick wall. "I have feelings for you that I don't want to have shut down simply because you think I can't handle instability. I have news for you: my entire world is unstable right now. I...I could be stuck on land forever. Away from my family and friends and everything I've known and loved.

Forever!" All the struggling finally wore me out, and I leaned against his chest. "My life has been spent in fear that what happened to my mother could happen to me, and now that fear has become a reality. My mother was stolen from me, and I saw the impact it had on my people and my father. Now I'm being held here on land by Murray." My legs grew weaker, but I kept myself upright. "You're the only thing in my life right now that is relatively stable. The only thing keeping me sane and making me feel like I'm not alone in the world. But you just want to push me away." I pulled back enough to look up into his eyes. "That hurts more than anything else I'm going through right now."

He sighed and squeezed his eyes shut for a moment. "If you only knew what I'd done, you wouldn't want me. I'm not the great guy you think I am. I'm a werewolf. I can be a true monster at times. I'm not some puppy dog that will lick your face and keep you warm at night. I have real regrets."

I brushed my hand against the strong line of his jaw. "We all do. I don't expect you to be anyone other than who you really are. Just like I'd hope you could accept me for who I am."

He leaned his face against my palm and placed his hand over mine. "That's the thing. I do accept you, but I'm not like Murray. I wouldn't want to hold you against your will, away from your family and everything you've ever known and loved. I want to think I'm a better man than that. You deserve better than to be deprived of your world. I don't know how we could be together. I can't stay here in Durness. I have obligations that require me to travel somewhere far away. I don't want to just drag you along for my pleasure when you're secretly in pain."

My lower lip trembled. I'd thought ill of him, when the reason why he wasn't keen to be with me was to protect me from heartache, not cause more. I blinked up at him, unable to find words.

I opened my mouth to respond, but he bent his head and brushed his lips against mine in a slow, sweet caress. I wrapped my arms around his neck, not wanting to let go. The kindness he had shown me made my heart race in my chest. He knew exactly what to do and say to make me feel alive and wanted, even if he was reluctant to let me into his life. And now that I knew how he felt, I could understand. I just didn't want to be pushed away, even if I understood why he didn't want to get too close to me. We could make this work. If it was still intact, I knew Colin would help me find my pelt. He was such a good guy that I wasn't sure I'd want to be without him, although I wondered as well how we'd manage to be together with our differences. I would always feel an affinity for the ocean and for water.

Now wasn't the time for those kinds of thoughts, though. First things first—we had to get back my pelt.

18

COLIN

I pulled Unna closer to me. I wasn't much for talking about my feelings, especially when I was already on the verge of losing control of my beast. This conversation wasn't doing much to help, but maybe it had been good to share with her. At least now we understood one another. She didn't need to get involved with an asshole like Murray who wouldn't appreciate her for the true gem she was. Granted, I very much doubted Ægir would do that either, but at least with him, she'd be amongst her people. She wouldn't be trapped on land, always longing for the connection with the sea she wouldn't really be able to have anymore. At least, that's the impression I got from what little selkie folklore I knew. We would need to discuss at some point how much of that folklore was true, and how much was fiction.

Right now, we had other things to deal with.

My priority was keeping her safe and getting her pelt back. I knew Murray worked for the fishery east of the village to get extra money for his boat repairs, and that he frequented the pub. That meant we might be able to investigate the selkies' cottage and his property without being disturbed. Or it might not be good, if he took the pelt with him during his work hours. If that were the case, I'd have to figure out his schedule, and we'd have to wait around while Unna grew more and more unsteady. She seemed more on edge than before, and I didn't want to watch her slip into a downward spiral. I'd seen what she was willing to do when she first lost her pelt. If she took drastic measures, I'd never be able to forgive myself. We had to get her pelt back as soon as possible. She was becoming far too precious to me to let anything bad happen to her.

I led her back into the house. Dark circles were beginning to form under her eyes, and I could tell she hadn't really slept. Besides, I'd fallen asleep by accident on that couch the first night, and it was horrendously uncomfortable. That was saying something, since I'd slept just fine on the ground outside and awoken well-rested.

"I never had a chance to ask about what you found out at the bar," she said, looping her arms around my waist as we stood in the living room. Her big blue eyes stared up at me expectantly. Thoughts of her looking up at me while we were naked and consummating our attraction toward one another nearly drove me to kiss her, but now wasn't the time. She needed to know what I'd learned.

But... Stop it. Keep yourself together. Your cock can wait.

I was surprised by the strength of my attraction, considering the full moon was still a few weeks away. The last one had occurred shortly before I returned to Scotland, and I'd managed to keep to myself during it. That hadn't been easy with my sex drive at a full roar, needing to be with any woman at all. But I hadn't trusted myself with either human or werewolf females. Now, though, I couldn't stop thinking about making love to Unna.

I cleared my throat and eased her back to arm's length.

"Sorry, I just need some space to concentrate. Being this close to you makes me... You're intoxicating." I ran a hand through my hair and looked over to the kitchen. Since meeting her on the beach, I hadn't even thought of alcohol, unlike before when I'd downed it at a rate unhealthy for the average human. "I spoke with the bartender from the pub. He gave me some details on Murray, and then when I was about to leave, I noticed Murray and one of his friends coming in. I...talked with him, and he's pretty adamant to have you back. I don't care. I'll do whatever it takes to protect you." I pulled the directions from my pocket to show her.

She smiled, but wrapped her arms around her torso as if hugging herself. "I'm glad you're safe. I was worried about you. When you didn't come back, I thought he might have hurt you." She laughed softly, and I enjoyed that sound very much.

I hadn't realized that she might worry about my safety. The chances of me being hurt weren't great. Hurting other people, especially Murray... Well, that was a different story. But I could handle myself. My concern was with keeping her protected. She was a selkie, but it didn't seem like she was much different from a human without her sealskin. I didn't want to see her hurt. I doubted she could withstand the kind of beating I could, and that thought frightened me.

"Ye dinnae have to worry about me. I'm much sturdier than I look. Murray wouldn't be able to hurt me so easily." I didn't know if I should tell her the whole truth about me. She thought she knew me, but if she knew just how unstable I was, would she still want to be with me?

"What is it?" She frowned and took a step closer. "You seemed like you were going to say more." The vixen was a little too perceptive for her own good.

I squeezed my hands into fists, then extended my fingers, trying to release some of my tension. It didn't help. "There's something you should probably know. I had a hard time controlling myself with Ægir. His arrogance and the way he treated you rubbed me the wrong way. But I've been through a lot lately, and like I said, I have regrets. Things I've done that I'm not pleased with. As a result, my wolf had become a little too dominant. Normally my beast is primal, and instinctual to an extent. Because of what happened, my wolf and I became more closely linked than normal, since he was all I had to hold onto. Now I'm struggling with him because he tries to take over and make me more beast than man."

I balled my hands into fists again, keeping them at my sides. It was all I could do to maintain eye contact with her. I hadn't told anyone how I felt or what was going on, not even my sister. Unna was the only one. I turned from her to put space between us.

"I'm unstable. There's another reason why I didn't want to get involved with you: if we became intimate, I might hurt you, physically hurt you. My beast could decide to take over, and… It's happened, and with my resolve so fragile, I don't want to put you in danger. Or be the reason werewolves are revealed to the world.

"My people dealt with that threat during the medieval times, and it was hard enough to handle then. These days, it'd be almost impossible for us to resume life. We're seen as a strong, bloodthirsty people. The place where I'm currently living, in America, is dealing with a situation that could have consequences for all werewolves. I don't want to be the reason the same thing starts happening here in Great Britain and Europe. I have a sister living in Scotland, and I wouldn't want anything to happen to her because I couldn't rein in my wolf." I turned to face her, expecting to see a look of horror or disgust on her face, but all I saw was concern and sympathy. My heart skipped a beat. She was more than I deserved.

She didn't seem to care that she was falling for someone damaged, but I hadn't told her all of it yet. I hadn't told her my biggest regrets—outside of believing I had a good, loving father who turned out to be an arsehole—which would probably haunt me for the rest of my life.

I could still hear the brunette's scream as my claws ripped through the flesh of her back. I'd heard her around the research facility later, and briefly saw her after the Southeastern Pack had rescued all of us, but I hadn't spoken to her or let her know I was the reason for her new, cursed life. Granted, she didn't seem too bothered. She'd found someone in the research facility: perhaps it had been her assigned mating partner. They'd learned not to get close enough to me to let me have my own, which probably contributed to my lack of control.

The one female they'd tried to pair with me had been injured during our copulation. I hated myself for what I'd done to those two women. However, being unable to quench my insatiable libido had been sheer torment. If I'd tried to assuage my needs alone, I could've rubbed my cock raw and still not been satisfied.

"Colin, talk to me. What else?" She didn't close the distance between us, but I knew she was just trying to give me my space while I worked through my feelings. All of this from a woman who'd had her pelt stolen and could be stranded on land for the rest of her life.

I slumped onto the sofa and rested my chin against my palms. "The reason for my instability… I was abducted from my home while I was overseas with my new Pack. Somehow they knew I was a werewolf, I'm not sure how exactly. Maybe someone spotted me while I was out running in the woods near my house or something, but that's not what matters. They brought me to a research facility and stuck me with needles, did all sorts of experiments."

She sat beside me and placed her hand on the sofa between us. I covered it with my own, happy for the cool touch of her skin. "During the full moon, my kind goes into a sort of sexual frenzy. It's not a need we can control. It affects our thinking, so we usually have lovers for those nights. The scientist didn't want me to mate since I'd injured a female during the mating thrall right after I was taken there. Plus I was too dangerous for them to get close to. I'd shown them I didn't like their experiments at all." I squeezed her hand softly, not wanting to say the next part but knowing I should.

"One night I was so angry to be there. People came into my room—two guys and an unconscious girl, though I didn't know she was unconscious at the time—and the guy pressed her against the bars to the cage they kept me in. I was having a hard time controlling my beast. I went to swipe at the man because I really didn't want them in my space, but I ended up clawing the woman instead. It was a gruesome scratch down her back, which nearly hit her spine. When I realized what I'd done, I disappeared back into the shadows to brood. But...I've ruined that girl's life. I just don't know how to tolerate myself, knowing she's a werewolf because of my own stupidity."

Unna squeezed my hand tighter and pulled me into her arms. "You can't keep beating yourself up about that. It won't do you any good."

"Believe me, I know." I nuzzled her neck, breathing in her fresh, feminine scent, which distantly reminded me of the waves. I pulled her into my arms and rested my head on her shoulder. My wolf liked having her close. She wasn't like the other females I'd been around and had sex with to quench my lust. We enjoyed just having her in our lives.

"We've...I've talked enough. You should rest now." I ran my thumb over the smooth line of her jaw and stared down at her pink lips. "I'll wake you in a few hours when I'm confident Murray is off to work. We'll go to your home first, then we can check his place. We shouldn't spend a lot of time there since we don't want him to realize we've been poking around."

"Okay." She leaned up and kissed my lips. Her arms wrapped around my neck, and I placed my hands on her waist. Need lit inside me, but I shook my head. Making out wasn't what we needed to do right now, even if I really wanted it. Once she rested, we could find her pelt.

I stood, scooping her into my arms. She didn't weigh much at all. It took all my strength not to carry her to the bedroom and lay her down, but instead I set her on her feet and nudged her toward my room. I needed to make a plan so nothing could go wrong when we left here to retrieve her sealskin.

It seemed unlikely that Murray would keep her pelt at the selkie house, unless he stayed there twenty-four-seven, which he clearly didn't since I'd seen him last night at the pub. He would know that she could return there to find it. So our best options were either Murray's house or his boat. Thank goodness Mike had given me directions to Murray's home. We might be able to find something there to lead us to the boat if it came down to it.

Unna took a few steps toward the bedroom before she stopped and turned to me. She gave me a sad smile that spoke of more pain than I ever wanted to see on her face. "Before I go… Like I said earlier, you're not the only one with regrets. When I was younger, my mother was taken in front of me. A fisherman had found her pelt on the beach— we didn't have a cottage then—and this was in the Faroe Islands where fishermen were told tales of the selkie often.

"She made me hide, and I watched her being taken away from behind a few rocks. I remained quiet, afraid they'd come after me next. For a few days I stayed there, unable to do anything but sit and stare at where my mother had stood, not wanting to move from that spot. My father and a few of his men came up onto land and found me. He searched all over the island for her, but he never found her. It broke him. He has never gone on land since." She stood there with her hands at her sides, looking incredibly vulnerable and bare before me. "If I'd acted sooner and gone for help, maybe she could have been saved and brought back to my father and me. It's something I'll have to live with for the rest of my life." She shifted her feet a little nervously. "I still have a hard time with the fact she's gone, but I've had to make myself move on. If I didn't, I couldn't enjoy the beauty still out there."

I closed the distance between us, unable to help myself. She'd been through a heart-breaking and traumatic event and still had the strength to go on with her life. I couldn't imagine the horror and pain she'd experienced. It made my heart open to her that much more, even if I was still nervous about letting her in. Talking with her had changed everything for me, and now that I knew this, it made me feel even luckier to have her with me. If she could recover, maybe I could as well. Granted, my healing process would be more unique due to my beast, but I already felt a change in him since meeting her.

"Thank you for telling me. I can't imagine what it was like to go through something like that. You're a brave lass." I pulled her into my arms and brushed my lips over hers. She shivered beneath me, and I took a step back, breaking the kiss. "I'll wake you in a few hours." I headed back to the couch, where I lay staring up at the ceiling and thinking about the caliber of woman I'd found. Maybe coming to Durness had been good for me as both a wolf and a man. I couldn't help smiling.

19

UNNA

*S*leep didn't come easily. After talking with Colin in the early morning hours, I kept tossing and turning. It didn't help that the pillow, blankets, and sheets all smelled of his delicious musky scent. Wrapping up in that smell was amazing, and I couldn't imagine a more relaxing way to spend the morning.

I managed to grab a few hours of sleep before I awoke with a start. My dreams had carried me back to the terrible moment my mother was taken away from me. Just because I was able to push it aside for the most part to function in my waking hours didn't mean I had totally worked through it. I might never, but at least the incident didn't cripple me with crushing anxiety anymore. I tiptoed down the hallway. I didn't see Colin at first, and I certainly didn't hear him. I wondered for a moment if he'd gone out, but then I spotted him.

Colin lay on the sofa as I walked into the living room. He glanced up, and his eyes ran over my body, drinking in my form. I shivered a little at the intensity in his gaze. Staying with him had been more turbulent than I'd anticipated, but I was happy to be here, even though the pull of the sea wore me down. If I knew my pelt was safe I'd be able to relax, but we still hadn't made a move on Murray yet.

However, Colin had news that Murray was going out to work at a fishery with his friends, so we'd be able to search through his house and my people's cottage without worrying about him being there. Colin didn't want to lose control again, and I was grateful he wasn't leaving anything to chance. I wasn't sure I wanted to see him get so close to the edge again. It had scared me seeing him that way with Ægir.

"Sleep well?" he asked, pushing into a sitting position to make room for me.

"Not really." I sat beside him and shook my head. He wrapped his arm around my shoulders, and I glanced up at him. "How about you?"

"No, I didn't either." He leaned in close to me, and I felt the warmth of his breath on my neck. "Maybe we can catch a few more winks before starting the day."

I raised an eyebrow at him, but wrapped my arms around his torso. "I'd like that." I rested my head against his chest, and he held onto me to keep me from falling off the sofa.

"This wasn't what I was thinking of, lass." He shifted so I was on top of him and then stood with me in his arms. "Let's take it back to the bed." He held me by my bottom and leaned in to kiss me.

I opened my lips for him, letting him kiss me fully, savoring the feeling of him like this. I felt the press of his hard shaft against my stomach as he lowered my feet to the floor. He was so rock solid. Moisture dampened my thighs at the thought of being with him so intimately. I wondered if this was how my parents had been when they were younger, feeling so vulnerable and yet so willing to embrace the other person.

I pulled my shirt over my head and glanced up at him. He

watched me as if he was ready to gobble me up. The intensity of it made me a little nervous and excited at the same time. I let the shirt fall to the floor beside us.

"You're beautiful, love." He ran his hand down my arm, then cupped my hip, pulling me close to him again. I leaned up against him, letting my bare chest press against his. He groaned and pulled me in for another kiss, ravaging my lips like a hungry wolf. He walked me back to the bed, pushing at my pants as we went, leaving me in only my underwear while he was still in his jeans. His T-shirt was most likely somewhere in the living room.

I didn't want to be the only one undressed. I pulled at his jeans too, sliding them off his slender hips. My hand brushed against bare skin as I did, and I pulled back for a moment to see his jutting erection. I blinked at him, wondering how I'd fit all of him inside me. I'd never mated before, and I'd never had a desire to until now. When I glanced back up at him, he was grinning.

"Like what ye see there?" he said, humor blatant in his voice.

I nodded, unable to find any words for what I was feeling. It was all so much. I reached down to touch him, wanting to experience all of this, but he pulled my hand away before I could.

"Not so fast. I want to get to know your body a little before you start touching me. I only have so much control. I wouldn't want to get too out of hand and ruin the moment for you." He leaned in to kiss my neck, letting me drift off into the pleasure of his breath and mouth on me. I relaxed into him, just enjoying the sensations.

He lowered me to the bed, his mouth traveling from my neck to my shoulder slowly, as if he wanted to savor every second and every inch of me. I leaned my head back and closed my eyes. I'd never experienced such warmth and care before in all my life. I'd been right to trust Colin. He'd told me I didn't have anything to worry about, that he'd take care of me, and he was holding true to his promise in more ways than I'd imagined.

His lips trailed toward my chest, and he licked a slow circle around my nipple before taking the sensitive bud into his mouth. I groaned at the sensation. I wanted him more than I'd wanted anything in a long time. He knew exactly how to light my body on fire. I'd never felt these kinds of sensations, and I wanted to delve deeper into this bliss he was showing me.

He sucked at my nipple for a moment as he pinched the other one between his thumb and index finger, making it harden into a peak. I arched into his touch, savoring the feeling of him toying with me, wanting so much more. This was like nothing I'd ever known before. My human body wasn't used to this—I was barely used to my human body. How could I ever go back to enjoying my selkie pelt after he showed me all these new and different emotions? I pushed those thoughts aside. I could worry about that later.

He licked his way over to my other breast in slow circles, sparking heat between my legs and setting my body on fire. I ran my fingers through his curly red hair, enjoying the silky strands in my hands. Everything about him was so wonderful. I couldn't imagine being with Ægir now. Even if I did get my pelt back, would I want to return to the sea? Or, more importantly, to Ægir?

I knew that I'd feel the constant pull back to the ocean, though, unless I married Colin and basically put myself into the same relationship I would've had with Murray. But Colin was nothing like Murray, I knew that well.

He looked up at me and pinched my nipple hard enough to bridge the gap between pleasure and pain. "What are ye thinking about? I want your attention where it should be: on this moment we're having together."

I smiled and looked down at him. "Sorry. I'm focused on us now. I promise."

He grinned that roguish smile at me, and pressed a few kisses over my chest before sliding down toward my stomach. "No worries, lass. If you weren't before, you will be soon."

I raised an eyebrow at him, wondering what he was talking about, until he drew his hands up my thighs and he slid a finger between my legs. I moaned and spread my legs for him, unable to believe the sensations he was able to cause within me. His thumb pressed onto my clit while his finger lightly circled my entrance. He hesitated for a moment, as though asking for permission. As if what we'd already been doing wasn't permission enough for this. I lifted my hips, urging him on.

"Please, Colin. I need your touch. I need this." My voice was so raspy I could hardly recognize it.

He speared me with his finger, and I moaned as he thrust it in and out as though it were actually his cock. He slowed down after a moment, drawing it out a little, but I knew that I couldn't take too much more. Pressure was building within me, and I felt like I was about to explode.

I clenched my hands in the bedsheets, desperate to have something to hold onto to anchor me.

He smiled, a knowing look in his eyes as if he was completely aware of the power he had over me. And yet, I wouldn't give away this moment for the world. Just being here with him was more than I could've ever asked for. If I'd known before I came on land that I would have my pelt stolen, and that Colin would be here to give me the love and caring he had, I'd gladly repeat my decisions.

He lowered himself between my legs, and blew out a

breath on my thighs. I bit my lip so hard I feared I might draw blood. He pressed kisses to my thighs and then to the soft, sensitive nub between my folds. I groaned as he nibbled on my clit briefly before alternating with firm, long strokes of his tongue. My body shook hard as waves of pleasure crashed through me. I screamed his name over and over again, unable to believe the intensity of my orgasm. "Colin, oh... Colin!"

My body trembled as he drew himself over me. I'd wondered why he hadn't taken any pleasure himself or consummated our relationship yet the way I knew humans did with one another. He grabbed a small square wrapper and rolled a condom on before he pressed himself against my entrance with his cock. "You're gorgeous, Unna. I can't imagine not being with you."

His words made me feel whole, like he was saying things I'd waited forever to hear, and I really had. I wanted the intimacy a relationship like ours could provide, but I knew I'd never be able to find it with Ægir or any of the other selkie men I knew. They were too utilitarian about relationships. They mated to fulfill the need to produce more selkies, instead of trying to find the kind of love I'd come to desire after seeing my mother and father's relationship.

"I can't imagine not being with you either," I said, my throat a little hoarse from crying out his name.

He leaned into me, kissing my neck here and there. I tilted my head to the side, enjoying the feeling of his mouth on my throat. I didn't consider him a threat, even if I had when we first met. I knew he was dangerous and a little scary, but he was also caring. I knew he wouldn't intentionally hurt me. He'd shown enough times that he was concerned about my wellbeing. After all, he had taken me in after Murray had chased me. He'd gone to the bar and confronted the man. He'd convinced me not to end my life when I'd been at my weakest. He'd proven himself time and again to be someone truly special.

He nudged himself a little farther inside me, going ever so slowly, as if I were made entirely of glass and one wrong move would break me. I appreciated his concern, since all of this was so new to me, but my body was on fire with need. If I didn't have him moving inside me, filling me completely, I might scream from the heavy desire weighing on me.

I pressed my hips against his, trying to thrust back onto him, but he just grabbed them and held me in place. I liked that he was taking control of the situation, but my body was alight and desperately in need of relief. More importantly, I wanted to share in the moment with him. The first orgasm had been delicious, but going it alone had been confusing and not at all what I'd hoped for. This was already making up for it, but I wanted both of us to enjoy it.

He slipped in further as his hand slid up my side, caressing my hip, my waist, and then over my stomach toward my thighs. He slipped his thumb between my folds again, nudging the sensitive bud he'd lavished earlier with his tongue. Circling my clit relentlessly, he stoked the flames in my body so high I thought I might combust.

He smirked, obviously pleased with my soft whimpers of pleasure. Rocking his hips until his cock was the rest of the way inside me, he held himself there for a moment to allow me to get used to his size. I ground my hips against him, and this time he wasn't able to stop me, since he was preoccupied with playing with my clit. He groaned, and I loved hearing just how aroused this made him. Then again, his enjoyment was visible, and I could feel how hard he was inside me as well.

Still, I craved him more, faster. My body was on fire. I wondered what it would be like to do this during his mating thralls. Would he lose control? Could he hurt me? He'd said he'd injured the female werewolf, but looking into his eyes, I could see just how much he cared for me. A guy like that wouldn't intentionally hurt me.

He rocked his hips harder against me, and I could tell he was losing some of his control. His body shook with pent-up frustration as he kept going, kept driving himself in thrust after thrust. It almost felt like he was trying to merge with me and become one. I loved it and didn't want this to stop, yet I also craved feeling the heights of pleasure again...this time with him inside me. Colin drew himself almost completely out before slamming in again, over and over, until I didn't know how much more I could handle. My climax was becoming a real, overbearing force that loomed over me, waiting to strike again. It was like sitting on a beach, looking up at a wall of water ready to crash over me and bury me in perfect bliss.

My body exploded with pleasure, and any control Colin had seemed to shatter. He let out a feral growl as he thrust into me harder than before. Pleasure and pain walked a fine line, as he fisted the bed on either side of my head and leaned his forehead against mine. I felt all of his muscles bunch up tight as he let out a harsh breath before very slowly relaxing. The muscles in his chest flexed, and I wanted to run my hands over that sweaty expanse, but I didn't know if I could, given how weak I felt after that amazing experience.

Colin kissed me, letting the brush of lips linger for a moment before he rolled onto his side. "That was incredible, lass."

"It was." I couldn't suppress the feeling of pride that swept through me when he said he'd enjoyed the encounter as much as I had, aside from the minor pain at the beginning. I didn't know if I wanted to ever get out of this bed again, especially not if he was in it. That thought dredged up the feelings of anxiety lingering in the back of my mind.

If I stayed with him, I'd never return to the sea, unless he asked me to, or unless I was able to outsmart him and steal back my pelt. If...I was able to get my pelt back. If I wasn't, I couldn't be sure I'd survive without it. Would I die if it were destroyed? Or would I be stuck living the rest of my life as a mere human? This form wasn't horrible, but I knew my existence wouldn't be a pleasant one if half of my soul was forever destroyed. As a selkie married to a man, I would be doing my duty, but without that...I pushed the thoughts out of my head. *Don't go there. Now isn't the time to dwell on those thoughts. You're probably overthinking things, anyway.*

I hoped I was right, because if that became a reality, maybe it would be better for the waves to take me back. I bit my lower lip and nuzzled Colin's chest, hoping he was able to help. My only chance of freedom depended on him. If I were left to fend for myself, I'd be forced into marriage with Murray.

20

COLIN

"We should go get your pelt back, love. Murray is bound to be gone now. It should be safe for us to retrieve it." I pulled her closer to me, pressing a kiss to the top of her head. I didn't want her to leave after we'd gotten her pelt back. Having her in my life meant more than I could have possibly imagined.

"Yes, we should." She leaned up and kissed me, placing her small hands on my bare chest. She was behaving differently after we made love, a lot more sensual than before. I enjoyed listening to her call my name, and the melodic foreign words she'd moaned were beautiful even if I didn't know what she was saying.

I pulled her on top of me so she was pressed against my already growing cock. If we didn't stop this soon, we'd probably stay in bed for who knew how long, but I didn't have a problem with that.

"We need to get going," Unna said, and reluctantly slid off of me. Her longing gaze lingered on my face for a moment before she turned to find her clothes. We stepped outside after getting dressed, and headed toward the cottage the selkies used. There was little to no wind in the air, and the morning sun shone from beneath an array of clouds.

Neither of us had a car, so we ended up walking. It wasn't too bad, but we made sure to keep a lookout in case Murray was around. Neither of us wanted to be taken by surprise. If anything, we were hoping to surprise him, or better yet, not even deal with him.

Upon reaching her cottage, we explored the outside, looking for signs that Murray or one of his friends might be around. From the smell of things, no one had been around for a while, but I wanted this to be handled well. Recklessness would only cause problems. I pushed all thoughts aside as we decided to head into the building.

We searched the house systematically, first checking the chest, which was still unlocked in the bedroom. We didn't find it anywhere. That led me to believe I was right. It wouldn't have been smart for him to keep it here. It didn't take long for us to be on our way, but I knew we'd need a car if we hoped to make this easier. Our first stop would have to be the pub.

The idea of walking through the Highlands bothered me a little. I'd rather run for that distance, but with Unna along, that was out of the question. We took a small shortcut through a nearby small forest to shorten the path by a few minutes. The refreshingly cool air helped me to clear my head. The forest was filled with all kind of familiar smells and sights, but Unna paid curious attention to our surroundings. Her eyes lit up as she stared at the branches above, where the red squirrels chased one another. The smile on her lips truly made my day and made it feel like anything was possible. I just hoped that feeling would last.

The road we got on took us directly to the town, and with everyone busy at work, there was little to no traffic around. The bar, open as always, was mostly vacant. Two of the older gentlemen I'd seen before were at their table in the corner. It seemed like they never left the pub. One of them didn't pay us much attention, while the other gave a cursory glance before he resumed reading his newspaper. Mike was wiping off the counter and tidying up behind the bar when we walked over. "Hello there, lad and lass, what will it be?" he asked, keeping his voice low.

"Hello, Mike. Thanks for your help. This is Unna, the lass Murray meant harm to. I wanted to say thank ye. We need to ask another favor of you." Mike was a decent fellow. I only hoped he'd be understanding and help us again.

There was some hesitation in his voice, and he tapped the bar in front of me. "You should order something." He glanced between the two of us, and I could see any uncertainty he had begin to melt away. He poured each of us a Scotch ale before disappearing into the kitchen. The help Mike had already given put me in debt to him, so I didn't say anything. If that cost me two beers, then two beers it was.

I took our drinks, and we wandered off to a table. We passed a little time by talking, while I kept my eye on the bar, hoping Mike would join us. I drank my ale relatively quickly, but it wasn't until Unna was nearly done that Mike walked over.

"So, lass, how may I be of assistance? I won't ask much, but if ye can, tell me what's going on." He looked between us, then resettled his gaze on Unna. "No offense, but I'd like to hear it from you," Mike said.

She blushed slightly, and I opened my mouth to comment. Before I could say anything, Unna replied, "Murray took something of mine. He's blackmailing me with it. If I don't stop him, he'll force me to marry him, and I trust my heart to someone else," she said, glancing in my direction. My wolf smelled the truth of her words, and my heart picked up its pace.

Mike looked between us again and broke into good-natured laughter. "Well, I can guess who that might be. My, my, Murray really has made himself a fool this time. There's scorn like that from a forced bride. So, how can I help you?" His accent grew thicker the more he spoke.

"Neither of us have transportation here. While I enjoy walking, we'd rather get this sorted out with Murray sooner than later. And ideally without him knowing. We need a car." I kept my voice neutral, even though my nerves were on edge. What if he said no?

"Of course...of course. Hmm... How long would you need it for?" Mike asked. "If I give up my wheels, I want to know I'll be able to go home tonight." He winked and slid his keys onto the table between us.

"We shouldn't be more than a few hours." The fact he'd actually loaned us his car was more than I could comprehend. I'd hoped he would agree, but this really meant something to me.

We thanked him profusely and headed out of the bar to his old pick-up truck. As we got in, my nose picked up numerous smells coming from it. Unna apparently didn't catch the foul scents, and I didn't want to tell her what had at one time or another happened in the very seats we were now sitting on. The engine started eagerly, though, and before long we had left Durness behind.

It took us half an hour to navigate the winding roads and arrive at Murray's home. Instead of just driving up to the house, we agreed to check the place out beforehand. I pulled the car to a shadowy corner along a group of trees, and we approached the house on foot, using their shade as cover.

I was suddenly very happy we'd agreed to inspect the place first when I caught sight of Murray hanging around on his porch. I'd hoped he would be gone by now, but instead, he entered the house. Remembering what Mike had shared about Murray, though, I knew it was only a matter of time before he'd be off to see his fishermen friends and head into town for a drink. "He should be leaving soon," I said to Unna, whose hands had curled into fists.

It seemed like the closer we came to Murray's home, the less she acted like herself. As if she was holding herself on a tighter leash.

I placed my hand on her shoulder, and she gave me a brave smile. We were both nervous about this—I could smell her anxiety—but we were getting closer to finding her sealskin. I knew that. As we sat in the cover of the trees waiting for our chance to strike, I pulled her into my arms. Her gaze remained set on his front door, so I wrapped my arms around her waist completely, in case she tried to jump up and rush toward the building.

With the scents she was giving off, it seemed like I might be the more stable of the two of us right now, and that prospect startled me. She was supposed to be my rock, but I guess that wasn't entirely fair. I would have to do what I could to keep us both under control.

21

UNNA

*S*itting there waiting for Murray to leave nearly drove me mad, but the part that scared me the most was how strongly I felt drawn toward the house—drawn toward him—like a puppet on a string. I had to hold myself in check, and it almost took physical effort to keep myself beside Colin. If I didn't, I would be endangering us. I knew Colin said that his loss of control could lead to more than just us getting hurt. He truly feared the idea that he might rip people to shreds and bring the existence of his kind to light, and I believed those weren't idle concerns.

I leaned my head against his chest, feeling close and safe with him even if I knew that the person who had caused me the most fear, outside of the fisherman who'd stolen away my mother, was right inside that house. I bit my lower lip, trying to keep it from trembling, and clenched my hands tighter into fists.

"Lass, you're working yourself up. Take a few deep breaths." Colin ran his hand over my hair in soothing motions. Once I got over my surprise that he was able to read me so easily, I looked up at him to see his amber eyes staring down at me.

My eyes widened, and it was all I could do to keep calm. Seeing the evidence of his wolf like that was something still pretty new to me. "Sorry, I..."

"You dinnae have to apologize. You're just working my beast up a little, and I'm already having problems with him. He's demanding I go inside and rip Murray to shreds, and it's pretty difficult to hold myself back, especially when you're beside me and so emotional. I know this is a lot for you to deal with. Just try to help me deal with it too." He kissed the top of my head, and I buried my nose in the crook of his neck, breathing in his scent. Just a sniff of his strong, masculine scent started to relax me and bring me back down to a calmer place.

My body sunk into his and I took a few more deep breaths, doing my best to keep more under control. I could relate to what he was feeling, since some of what I felt was due to Murray's magical control over me. That's the way selkie magic handled a human having control over a selkie: it kept us in our place, for lack of a better term.

Several more minutes passed, and I kept my relative calm by focusing solely on my breathing, nothing more. If I could just breathe in and out, then I'd survive this. That's all my world focused in on.

Colin relaxed a little beside me, and I realized just how tense I'd made him. Ugh... I didn't need to be a distraction to him, not when so much was on the line. Not only my pelt, but our relationship and my future. I had to do my part and pull my weight in this.

I was so relaxed after a while of focused breathing that I was nearly asleep. I couldn't believe that I'd gotten so comfortable in his presence as to nearly take a nap while we were staking out Murray's house. I closed my eyes for a moment, but it didn't last. The second I did, I heard a door slam.

Colin placed his hand over my mouth as I bolted upright, making a soft squeak. "Ssshhh... We can't draw attention to ourselves. We're not that far from him, and he could still hear us." He pressed another kiss to the top of my head, and I nodded to let him know I understood. He slowly removed his hand from my mouth and moved into a crouch. He looked ready to pounce at a moment's notice, and I was so with him. If we could get my sealskin back, I'd be forever grateful.

Murray got into his truck and pulled out of his small driveway, going off toward town and most likely the pub. It was around lunch when I'd first met him and saw him with his friends there. It made sense that he'd be leaving right now.

I started to climb to my feet, but Colin placed his hand on my shoulder. "Not yet. We shouldn't go just yet. Give him five minutes to make sure he doesn't come back for some reason. We don't want to get caught doing this if we can help it. I could handle him, but I don't want to be put in that position. I...I dinnae think I could just fight him enough to get the pelt and get out of there. I'm scared I might kill him. If that happened, I could very well lose complete control of my beast."

"You won't," I said. "I believe in you. You're stronger than you give yourself credit for." I smiled at him, and he gave me a half-smile in return. It lit up his eyes a little, but he didn't seem like he believed me.

"Ye believe in me more than I believe in myself. Let's just hope we don't have to find out. I'm not sure I'd want to go there." He turned his head back to the road and kept watch for Murray returning.

We stayed back in the trees for five minutes, but Murray

didn't come back. We were ready to go. Colin rose completely to his feet and helped me to mine. The good thing about this area was that the houses weren't completely beside one another. Closer to town they were more tightly grouped, but Murray lived out in the countryside. He probably liked his privacy, or maybe it was a family home. I didn't know and didn't care.

Colin grabbed the key from where Murray had hidden it, and then handed it to me for safe keeping. I didn't feel quite the pull toward the house that I had before, and I wondered if it was tied to Murray now. I'd never had my pelt stolen before, obviously, and I hadn't looked into the mechanics of how the magic worked. Did it focus on my pelt or him? I should've learned more about it when my mother was taken, but I'd been too focused on the pain I was dealing with. I hadn't cared how it worked. All I knew was that I wanted to avoid it at all costs. Now I could see how silly I'd been.

Regardless, we had the house to ourselves for a moment to sift through and see what we could learn. If we found it here, great. If not, we might see where else he could be hiding it. How many places could he have to stash it? There couldn't be that many, could there?

My stomach ached at the thought. He had friends who might be willing to help him either get rid of it or hide it. Maybe I should just surrender myself. I wrapped my arms around myself as Colin unlocked the door. I glanced around the wide-open space around us to make sure we were alone.

Colin glanced in my direction, and I took a few deep breaths, trying not to project my discomfort at being there. We needed to stay focused, and he couldn't do that if I was casting off all kinds of emotions at him and his wolf.

He grinned at me, and I wondered if it was that noticeable a change for him, when I relaxed versus when I was upset. I wasn't sure I liked him knowing exactly how I felt, but I could dwell on that later, when we weren't breaking into someone's home. Or at least letting ourselves in.

"Come on. Let's get inside and get this done and over with." He held out his hand to me, and I took his. He led us in and closed the door behind me. The place smelled horrible, like fish, body odor, and alcohol. There were beer bottles, cans, and bottles of whiskey everywhere. He wasn't one for keeping his space clean.

I stepped over some kind of small animal skeleton, and I cringed. I drew closer to Colin, not wanting to be very far from him all the sudden.

"God, this guy needs a maid. It smells foul." He pinched his nose, but I wasn't sure that would help much. "You check the living room, dining room, and kitchen. I'll look toward the back of the house."

I watched him step over the bottles as he made his way back. I didn't want to be here anymore. I looked to the living room, sighed, and instantly regretted the intake of air. There was a box of tissues on the couch and several wadded-up ones on the floor, like someone had a cold recently. When I stepped closer, I smelled stale semen. No, not a cold. On the coffee table were several magazines as well as DVDs with naked women on the covers. I moved away from them, unable to believe I'd actually let this person into my people's cabin. How stupid had I been? I wanted to cry...and puke. It took everything I had within me not to.

There weren't any spaces I could see where he could be hiding something like my pelt. A quick peek under the couch showed nothing but an army of dust bunnies, and all the other places to check were also filthy, like they hadn't been cleaned in years. There was no way he'd hid anything there recently.

I looked around, unwilling to touch anything I didn't

have to. As I walked back into the living room, I twisted my ankle on a beer bottle and bit my lip hard against a cry of pain. I didn't want to startle Colin and distract him from his search. Neither of us knew when Murray would be back, and we had to make sure we checked the entire house. We couldn't leave without being certain we had given it our best shot. I searched the living room, the kitchen, and the dining room, but all I turned up was lots of clutter and filth.

I started toward the back of the house, where Colin had disappeared, but he walked out of the hallway holding something. I nodded toward the slip of paper. "What did you find?"

He looked me over, and I stood up straighter, making sure I didn't move so he couldn't see the slight limp I'd picked up. "Not what we were hoping to find. Murray is one twisted person, who could use some cleaning tips. But I have an idea where we can check next."

He held out the piece of paper to me. It looked like a receipt of some kind. "Mike told me that Murray's boat is currently being repaired. That's the dock where it's being worked on. That's one place he might not expect people to go looking for your pelt."

My heart burst with excitement. Colin was right. I hadn't even thought to look there, but it was a great idea. Murray was a fisherman, and the place he most cared for was his boat. He'd shown pride in his profession when we'd talked. "Yes, you're right. We should go look." I smiled at him and wrapped my arms around him in a big hug.

"The address is on here. If Murray is still off at the pub, we should have time to go by and take a look real quick. We'll have to be fast, since I don't want to give them the chance to catch us off-guard, but if we're right, you'll be back to the sea tonight." Colin gave me a sad smile, and I could feel his pain. Those words drew me down too. I loved that I could go back to the sea and be with my father again, but after being with Colin, I didn't necessarily want that as badly anymore. I wanted to be with him. I just wasn't sure how that would work out.

I placed my hand on his and nodded, returning his regretful expression. "Guess so." Then we left, and I locked the door before sliding the key back under the welcome mat just as Murray had left it, covering our tracks.

UNNA

*W*hat Colin said at Murray's bothered me the whole way to the docks, even though I knew he didn't mean it in a bad way. I knew he was only trying to be helpful by saying if all went well tonight I would be returning to the water, but that's not what I wanted, exactly. What I wanted was to be with him. Hadn't we talked about this?

I stared out the passenger-side window and remained quiet. Getting into an argument wouldn't help either of us, but the silence between us was tense, as if we were both waiting for all of this to blow up in our faces.

Getting to the docks took longer than we'd expected. Thankfully we had Mike's truck or else the walk there would've been hellish for me. Colin probably would've been fine, but my feet still hurt from the trek to the pub, which was a decent bit away from my people's cabin. I'd tried to push the pain aside—the alcohol had helped a little—but this was easily double or quadruple that distance. It didn't help that neither of us were familiar with this area. All the time I'd spent in Scotland had been on this trip or viewing it from the water. Colin had lived south of here, and now resided in some other location he hadn't told me about yet. All he'd mentioned was how far away it was, but I wanted to know more. I knew this wasn't the time to push him on it, though.

Colin parked a little ways off in case someone came around to investigate. There weren't many other boats or people around here, so it would be easy to draw unwanted attention to ourselves. We had to be careful and cautious. Just a couple people checking up on our boat, not strangers snooping around where they weren't wanted.

I climbed out of the truck and looked around at our surroundings. A few people were working on a boat off toward the back of the docks, but I didn't recognize them as Murray's friends from the pub. Besides, they appeared to be wrapping things up. Maybe they'd leave soon and we would have the place to ourselves to figure out which boat was Murray's. The receipt hadn't given us any obvious clues, but maybe we missed something.

Colin held out his hand to keep me from walking toward the docks. Frowning, I followed his gaze. The men who were working on the boat watched us for a moment before going back to their business as if we weren't worthy of notice.

I let out a sigh of relief and slumped a little against the car. I pulled the receipt from my pocket again, wanting to double-check it before we ventured closer. It had a tally of the money owed and descriptions of the charges, but now that I looked, it also mentioned something about touching up the paint on the boat's name: "Big Rosie." I don't know how we'd missed that earlier.

I looked up again, scanning the different boats. Toward the other side of docks from the two men, also in the back and closest to the water, I spotted the boat in question. I took a few steps toward Colin. He was still searching our surroundings as if expecting something or someone to jump out at us at any minute. I couldn't blame him, though, since I kept expecting this all to go downhill fast, but I had to think positively or I might make a mistake that could cost us.

"I found Murray's boat," I said, keeping my voice low. I doubted the men over there could hear us, unless they were supernatural beings like Colin, but I didn't want to take any chances.

He looked over at me for one of the first times since we'd arrived here. "How?" He glanced back at the paper in my hands, then up to my face. "We looked over that."

"But we missed this." I pointed toward the bottom where the comments mentioned fixing the boat's name.

He took the paper from me and nodded. "Good catch." He handed it back, then started off toward the boat as if he had every right to be there. The men were heading down to their car now. They waved at us, and I lifted my hand, unsure what else to do. They looked like fishermen, and I really didn't like anyone connected with that profession, especially after my mother being taken and then Murray trying to wed me. If it weren't for Colin, I'd be in big trouble.

He grabbed my hand and pulled me after him. He was walking swiftly, nearly dragging me along to make me keep up. I tried to lengthen my stride, but that didn't work, so I moved my legs faster until I was almost running just to keep up. "Sorry, Unna. I'm just not getting a very good feeling. Those guys seem like the type who knows everyone else who works here. We're the odd ones out. They might contact someone, so we have to search and get what we came for and then get the fuck out."

I frowned and threw a glance over my shoulder real quick. "They seemed pretty nice to me. I don't know what you mean." But I caught them still watching us and looking at one another. One of the men pulled out a small device, and pressed a few buttons on it. He held it to his ear and started talking. A mobile phone? My mouth dropped open a little, and I almost asked Colin about it, but my foot hit a bump and I fell into his back.

He grabbed me around the waist, pulling me to him until I was steady. "Keep up. We dinnae have much time." He looked over at them, then lifted me onto Murray's boat. "Start searching."

Suddenly I felt a surge of power hit me like a tidal wave. It dropped me to my knees. It was the most familiar feeling in the world, like gliding through the depths of the ocean. That slick, wet feeling on my skin, and the coziness of the cool darkness of the waves. My pelt! It was close by.

"Are you all right, Unna?" Colin placed his hands on me, but I pushed him away. I needed to concentrate now more than ever before in my life.

I closed my eyes, trying to feel where the pull of magic was coming from. There were so many small compartments on the boat that I didn't even know where to begin looking, but if I could follow the trail of magic, it might help. At least I hoped that was how it worked.

The longer I searched for it with my thoughts and the power within me, the more I could tell that it wasn't happening the way I'd hoped. There was no magical arrow pointing at my pelt telling me exactly where it was. If I'd been paying more attention previously, I probably would've felt the tug of it here on this boat, but there was only so far it could take me. I had to do the rest of the searching myself.

I opened my eyes and looked up at Colin. He was glancing between me and the guys standing by their cars in the small parking lot. They weren't moving yet, but the one guy was still talking on his phone. I couldn't hear what he was saying, but I figured Colin probably could from the sheer intensity of his gaze as he looked over at them. I didn't want to break his concentration, so I started rummaging through the boat, not even trying to hide my search. I didn't care if they found us out so long as we weren't present when that happened. But they were fishermen, with deadly gear, and there were a lot of sharp objects that looked dangerous if we went about this carelessly.

I shivered, wondering if they had caught any of my selkie kin in their nets, but I couldn't get distracted by that right now. Those thoughts could haunt me another time. Right now, I had to find the pelt so we could get out of here. I wasn't finding it on the deck, so I walked deeper into the boat. "I'm going below to see if it's there."

"Fine. Let's both go. It's better if we stick together." Colin looked to me. "But be careful. We don't want to be getting hurt on any of their tools here." He followed me down the steep ladder and into the small room in the lower section of the boat. It smelled just like Murray's house: stinky with the scent of body odor, fish, and even piss. I tried to hold my breath as much as I could, but I knew that I'd need a shower after having gone into these two places today. I wished for a moment that I could dive into the ocean to rid myself of the scents clogging my nose.

I headed to a small section with bunk beds and dug through there, pulling off blankets and feeling for any strange bumps. Reluctantly, I took a deep breath, hoping to catch any sign of my selkie pelt. Fortunately or unfortunately, my good sense of smell in selkie form didn't necessarily translate to my human form. Or maybe it was just overwhelmed with body odor and fish. In selkie form, I loved fish. But this fish just smelled...fishy and disgusting.

I leaned forward, propping myself up a little against the small table where they probably ate their meals. I noticed that the bench appeared to have hinges. I frowned. Could that be too obvious?

Colin pulled down several books from a shelf behind me,

and I cringed at the noise. He'd gone almost feral in his search. It kind of scared me, but I took another deep breath, trying to smell as little as possible, then let it out slowly. It didn't really help me calm down, but at least I was focused.

I pushed the bench up to find some yellow raincoats. My heart fell into my stomach, and I ran a hand through my hair, feeling like it was all futile. Then one of the raincoats shifted a little, revealing the edge of a shiny, black, almost rubbery material beneath it. My heart raced in my chest, and I pushed aside the raincoats and carefully lifted my selkie pelt from the compartment. I felt a surge of energy and wholeness. Joy filled me, and I wanted to scream my victory and jump up and down. The urge to put my skin on and dive into the water was overpowering, but I pushed it down. "Found it," I said, turning to face Colin.

Footsteps sounded on the deck above us, and I looked around for a place to hide. The men had seen us come in here, though. It'd be pointless to pretend otherwise. If we were going to get out of here, we had to fight. But Colin's eyes were already wolf amber, and I saw just how out of it he was. How could we survive, while still keeping his secret safe from the world at large?

My stomach knotted up at the thoughts shifting through my head. God. More than ever, I wanted to flee back to the water, but I didn't want to leave Colin. He meant a lot to me, and if it weren't for him, I wouldn't have my sealskin back. I'd really started to doubt I would ever see it again. I still wasn't sure if it was all in one piece, but from what I saw of it, it looked good enough to get me back in the water. With it being this whole, any minor scrapes would be repairable. My people knew how to magically heal the skin so a selkie man or woman would be able to continue on with their underwater lives.

Colin put himself in front of me, blocking me from the

entrance, or more likely blocking the men coming down the ladder from getting to me. My heart dropped in my chest when I saw the first man coming down.

Murray...

No. It couldn't be. Why was he here? Wasn't he supposed to have gone home afterward? Maybe we'd both been wrong, and he'd decided to visit with his friends to fix up the boat. Maybe he was just suspicious and thought we would be here. The two men up there might have called him.

"Let her go," Colin growled...yes, growled...in the most animalistic voice I'd ever heard. I almost didn't recognize his words.

"What do we have here? It's you again." Murray either didn't seem to notice the way Colin was acting, or he didn't care. He was messing with something far beyond him, but the one I cared more about right now was Colin. He couldn't lose control. He was so close to losing himself entirely to his beast. It might be his death, or at least the death of his human self, if he killed someone.

I placed my hand lightly on Colin's back. He tensed every muscle, and for a moment, I thought he would whirl on me. He didn't, but I knew I should remove my hand. I wasn't helping the situation by trying to intervene.

"Murray. Just let us go. I have my pelt back. You know the lore. I am free to return to the water." Even as I said it, my heart rebelled. I didn't really want to go back...at least not just yet. I wanted to explore what I had with Colin. If it didn't work out, I'd tell him so and we'd part. But it would be nice to tell my father so he didn't worry about me. I didn't want him to lack closure and relive what happened to my mother, constantly thinking I could be dead. That would rip me to shreds.

"You're not leaving here at all, lass. If you want to keep your boy-toy alive, you'll put that pelt back in the cupboard and get over here. You will be my wife whether you want it or not. I deserve respect amongst my family and friends. They always tell me I need to grow up and find a woman. Well, I've found one, and you're it." He waved me over to him, but I refused to go.

The man behind Murray pointed a gun toward us, and I bit my lower lip. Fear curled in my gut, and I wanted to hide. Colin went completely still. Even werewolves weren't immune to bullets, I guessed.

23

COLIN

y gut clenched at the sight of the gun. This situation had gone from inconvenient to terrible. While I knew I could survive a gunshot, I didn't think the same could be said for Unna. I didn't want to chance it either way. She meant too much to me. She'd finally gotten her pelt back, and I didn't want her to die now that she had. I fought the urge to look back at her, too afraid that Murray and his friend might decide to pull something if I did.

I put my hands in the air, trying to placate the two of them. They didn't know what I was. For all they knew I was some human who wanted Unna for myself. That's what Murray had implied when I met with him at the pub, anyway. "Just calm down. There's no need for guns here."

Murray just rolled his eyes and tried to walk by me, but the cabin space down here was too tight for that. He'd have to brush past, and while he might be acting brave, I had a feeling he could sense my predatory vibes. There was something about the way he positioned himself and glanced over at me, as if trying to measure up how tough I would be to bring down.

I tried to hide my grin, with some success, but that didn't matter. He was acting like a badarse, but he was scared of me. I could use that to my advantage.

I heard Unna move closer behind me. She placed her hand on my lower back. I felt the brush of the pelt there too, and I wondered what she was thinking. If we made it to land or at least the deck of the ship, how long would it take her to put it on and get away from here? I hoped not long. As much as I wanted to be with her, she should be back in the water with her own people. I hated the fact she'd be gone, though. The one lass in my life that I'd truly felt something for would be only a memory.

She moved back a little, as if realizing that she'd just put her pelt in closer proximity to Murray. But I wouldn't let him take it from her. I was faster than him. The only thing I wasn't confident about beating was the speeding bullet from the glowering man's gun. He kept staring at me as if wondering when he'd get to use it. Bloody hell.

"Come over here, Unna. If you don't, I'll have my man shoot this idiot." He frowned at her from over my shoulder. "Dinnae test me. If you have any doubts whether I'd do it, you only have to look at my face." I could tell he was dead serious. A gunshot wound would impact me, but I was reasonably confident that if he did shoot me, I could take the two of them out before they could harm Unna. Any more, though, and I wasn't sure, especially if they had guns.

As if on cue, I heard more footsteps on the deck above us, and I groaned under my breath. Damn it all. Why did I have to jinx us, even in my thoughts? This whole situation was really starting to enrage me and my wolf. For a moment, we wondered if giving into our desire to kill them all would be such a bad thing. After all, they were trying to hurt the female we cared for and swore to protect. But I knew it was just another trick to get me to lose control. While my wolf did care for her, he also wanted to get the upper hand on me, and I had too much to live for now to let him take me over like that.

I wouldn't be the same man if my wolf was fully set free. I took a deep breath, just trying to remain calm. I could tell from the slight twitch in the gunman's trigger finger that if something didn't happen soon, he might take things into his own hands prematurely.

"Unna, just go to Murray. It's okay." I tried to keep my voice as calm and as reasonable as possible. If we pretended to do as he asked, he might let down his guard. At least we would be in less danger from Mr. Itchy-Trigger-Finger, if I was reading the situation right. I just hoped I wasn't leading us into something worse.

Unna set the pelt down on the table behind me, then slowly inched her way toward Murray. I caught a quick look at her face, and she frowned at me intensely as if I'd betrayed her. Did she really think I'd give her up so easily?

I gave an almost imperceptible shake of my head. I wanted to tell her she would be safe and that I had a plan, but Murray and his friend couldn't know. Instead, I just stood there, watching her. I took a slight step backward, still keeping my arms up a little. The men were both watching Unna as if she might pull something, but I didn't want to give anything away. This was a risk, because Unna could be hurt without my body blocking the gun for her.

"You have her, now just let her go. I'm sure you can find another girl. You're a good-looking chap who makes an honest living." I didn't exactly mean it. He did make an honest living, but he stunk to high heaven of piss, fish, and other things. Not to mention he was a psycho who took women captive when he didn't get his way. I didn't think any woman would like being in a relationship with someone like that. At least none of the women I knew.

"No, mate. You have no idea what I'm about. In case you didn't hear what I said before, she's going to be my bride. She will be the woman I keep to take care of me, bear my children, and teach my parents that I'm not worthless. I can find a woman regardless of what they might think." He puffed out his chest, as if finding Unna and forcing her into a relationship was some noble quest that he'd won.

"That doesn't make ye worthy of her affection. You're kidnapping her, for Christ's sakes. She's not in love with ye." I instantly knew it was the wrong thing to say, but it slipped out before I could stop myself.

Murray backhanded me across the mouth, and I reeled back, more in surprise than in pain. He hadn't even punched me. He'd just slapped me. This was definitely a guy more used to picking on women than going up against other men. It brought back images of my father, and how my sister couldn't even get out the words to tell me what he'd done to her.

A surge of anger spread through my gut like wildfire, catching everything in its path. He wouldn't get away with hurting women. No woman deserved that kind of treatment.

"You have no say in my relationship with her. She's coming to me of her own free will. Isn't that right, Unna?" Murray held out his hand to her. When she didn't take it, he waved it a little.

Her gaze flicked between me and him, indecision in her eyes. I knew she didn't want to do it, and I didn't want her to either. I bit the inside of my cheek. The sound of footsteps on the ladder drew Murray's attention for a moment, and I shoved him into his friend with the gun. The gun clattered to the floor, and I kicked it away from them.

We needed to get out of this tight space before my werewolf went truly mad. I grabbed the leg of the man who was climbing down the ladder and pulled him onto his friends. They all groaned in pain at the sudden pile-up. Part of me wanted to put Unna on the ladder and get her out first, but I knew there was a man still up there, and I couldn't be sure if he had a gun too.

The men down here were starting to rouse, though. We couldn't stay here forever, and three of them versus her wasn't something I wanted to risk. I glanced over at her. She was near the table again, hovering over her pelt and looking truly unsure.

"Come on, lass. We need to get out of here." I nodded toward the ladder and held out my hand to her. "Let's go."

She grabbed the pelt at the last moment and darted to me. I grabbed her and set her high on the ladder. She climbed up, with me close behind. When she'd almost made it all the way up, she stopped, not completely blocking the ladder, but enough that I couldn't come the rest of the way up unless I pushed her aside. She clutched the pelt tighter to her chest and stared just out of my range of sight.

I remembered the footsteps earlier and grimaced, wishing I'd gone up first. But she was away from Murray and his friends, at least. I glanced down at the small room to see the men slowly climbing to their feet. "What's going on, Unna?" I asked.

She spared me a quick glance. "More men. One guy has a gun and the other...I'm not sure." Her lower lip trembled, and she took a few steps away from the ladder now as if to put distance between her and them. "Don't come any closer," she said to them.

"This must be Murray's lass. Grab her, Finlay. Let's get her into the truck and take her back to his place, so we can get back to the bar. I'm tired of cleaning up after that arse.

145

First he wrecks the boat, and now thinks he has something to prove to everyone with this shite."

Another man stepped forward as a hand wrapped around my ankle. I looked down to see the one I'd thrown off the ladder holding onto me. I used my other leg to kick him in the face. A loud crack sounded as I'm sure I broke his nose, and he lunged back, holding his face. Blood trailed down from under his hands, and I shook my head. Humans.

I climbed the ladder quickly, making it up just as the man with the gun approached Unna. I punched him in the wrist, sending the gun flying off to the back of the boat. He held his wrist for a moment, as if shocked that I'd come up from the belly of the ship and hit him. Then he got into a fighting stance and narrowed his eyes at me. I knew I'd quickly win this battle, but winning wasn't my true objective right now. What I wanted most was to get Unna out of here unharmed. If we managed that, I'd be packing my things and calling the cottage's landlady to tell her I had to wrap up my trip earlier than expected.

The man punched me in the jaw, but it barely hurt me. I stared at him, and he shook his hand as if shocked I didn't react to a punch that apparently hurt him to throw. "What the fuck? You must be hyped up on some kind of drugs, kid. PCP or something."

I grinned at him. If that's what he wanted to think, then it was fine with me. At least it skewed his perception of what I really was. Let him think I was a druggie. I didn't care, so long as we got out of here.

Clattering footsteps on the ladder drew my attention, and I looked over to see the first gunman starting to peek out of the hole. I made a move for him as his gun cleared the doorway, but the man I was brawling with shoved me really hard. This time, I stumbled toward the gunman, which startled him even more.

"Colin!" Unna's cries drew my gaze. I seriously didn't want her to get shot. I tried to balance myself and lunge for her, but it didn't work out that way.

The loud bang of the gun sounded shortly before a blast of pain hit my shoulder. I bit back a growl as I looked up at the gunman, and something changed in his face. I saw true terror. I lunged for him, but he must've let go of the ladder in his fear. He dropped down to the bottom and took out the guy whose nose I'd busted.

Pain pierced my side, and I yelled before I could stop myself. The man who'd punched me held out a bloody knife. He went to stab me in the side again, but I caught his wrist and twisted quickly, effectively snapping the bones and tendons within it. I shoved him away from me, and he jumped from the boat to the dock. He seemed truly frightened, so I didn't worry about chasing after him. Besides, having to worry about four others now was better than five.

My beast was already starting to take over from the violence and pain, but the overwhelming need to protect Unna at all costs kept me grounded, even if we hurt badly. She cried out, and I looked to see her near the boat's edge. The gunman was trying to grab her pelt away from her, but she was punching and kicking him. He threw a punch at her, hitting her in the face probably harder than he'd intended to.

Her body went limp, and she toppled over the edge of the boat, pelt and all.

My heart hammered in my chest, and I lunged toward where she'd been thrown overboard. Murray grabbed me by the arm and spun me to face him. I stopped suddenly, feeling the sudden desire—need—to rip his throat open. If it wasn't for him, she wouldn't be in this situation. He was the reason her pelt had been taken, the reason we had people holding knives and guns on us.

I squeezed my hands into fists. "Your man threw her into the water. Don't you want to save her?"

Murray narrowed his eyes at me as if I were telling some kind of sick joke, but he looked to the other man, and then scanned the rest of the boat. "Shite. What the bloody hell were you thinking, you idiot?" He came up beside me to the edge of the boat, and I wanted so much to snap his neck and throw his body into the water, especially while he wasn't paying much attention. But I had more important concerns.

I dove over the side of the boat into the cold water below. I was out of practice at swimming, but I'd been adept enough once. I saw her and her pelt drifting away from me, and my heart hammered in my chest. I swam harder, doing my best to reach her. She couldn't drown. I wouldn't let her die at the bottom of the bay. Not after I'd come to truly appreciate who she was to me. I truly cared for her. I didn't know what the future would hold, only that I wanted her in mine.

I pushed my body to the limits and finally caught hold of her ankle, then pulled her into my arms. I kicked my legs to swim up to the surface of the water. My lungs ached, and my oxygen was running out fast. I'd been fairly good at swimming before, and now I had a reason to get into the water more. We broke the surface of the water, and I looked down at her. Her lips had a faint blue tinge to them and she wasn't moving. I heard yelling above us on the ship, and I glanced up to see Murray looking absolutely distraught.

"Hand her up to me. She needs medical treatment. I know first aid." Murray waved to me. He had to be joking if he thought I'd do that. I wouldn't let him get anywhere near her, not after he'd had his men come around with guns and knives. I looked around and saw the shore, but it was further away from us than the boat. Guess I didn't have much of a choice. I looked down at her. Her lips were turning a deeper blue, and her pale skin was nearly translucent. I growled under my breath and lifted her from the water up to Murray.

He grabbed her under the arms, but he had a little trouble pulling her up. He called to his friend, and together they finally got her into the boat. Weakling. She barely weighed anything at all.

I treaded water for a moment, maybe expecting he would give me a hand up too, but it never came. They disappeared over the side with her, and I heard Murray grumble at his friend that he better actually be doing CPR, not kissing her. My beast raged in my chest at the thought of them being incompetent with her in such a fragile state. I grabbed a strap hanging over the side of the boat and jerked myself up, landing on the rim.

The men jerked back and stared at me, fear and concern in their eyes. Unna still lay there lifelessly. I grabbed Murray and his friend by their collars and threw them overboard. The rapid beat of footsteps on the dock drew my attention, and I saw the ones who had been downstairs now running to their cars.

I dropped to my knees beside Unna as Murray and his friend splashed around in the water.

"Fucking arse," Murray yelled. They were frantically treading water. They were fishermen—surely, they knew how to swim. Though I honestly didn't care if they drowned. They were as good as dead to me.

I breathed into Unna's mouth and tried to perform CPR as best I could. I'd trained in it a little in high school when I'd wanted to be a lifeguard, but that had been a long time ago. My pulse raced faster the longer she was unconscious. She couldn't die on me. I didn't want to hurt her, but I didn't want to lose her either.

All of a sudden, there was a large splash outside the boat, and I heard the two men scream bloody murder and the splashing intensified as if they were being attacked. Then all was silent. I thought about going to see what happened, but I had more important things to worry about right now. A slap of something wet hit the deck, and I jerked my head around to see a large grey seal on the boat. I kept myself low to the ground, sure this wasn't just a normal seal. This was a predator. It didn't look totally like the one I'd seen while at the beach: it seemed much bigger, though I couldn't be sure since that one had been much farther out. This one held itself with authority and power.

I moved to the other side of Unna, revealing her still body to the seal. It gave a roar of pain and darted toward us. With a flicker of magic, it became an older human man who was naked from the waist up. His pelt covered his legs, but didn't slow him down. "Did you do this?" he barked at me.

"No, the two men in the water did." I looked closer at him, seeing lines around his eyes and mouth, though he didn't look very old. Maybe mid-thirties or early forties. They appeared to be more from sadness than age. Then again, I didn't know how selkies aged. "You're her father."

"Yes." He held his hands over her chest and closed his eyes, chanting a few words under his breath in a melodic language I didn't understand. The power of the magic made me involuntarily jerk away from her. He bent his head closer. "Wake up, Unna. Come back to me, my daughter."

Her body jerked, and water spilled from her mouth. I dropped back down and rolled her to her side, not caring that her father was giving me hateful glares. The only thing I cared about was her living. "Aye, that's it. Spit out the water."

She coughed it all up, her body shaking with the effort. She slowly pushed into a sitting position and rested her head in her hands. I placed my hand on her shoulder to keep her steady, but her father brushed it away, pulling her closer to him.

"She's none of your concern now, human—" He narrowed his eyes at me, looking a little confused. "No. You're not a human, but what are you?"

"Father? You're here?" She wrapped her arms around him and rested her head on his wet chest. My beast wanted her curled up against me instead, but we knew she'd probably head back to the ocean now that she was with her family. "He's a werewolf."

"A werewolf? How strange. I thought they were beasts of myth." He looked intrigued, but shook his head as if dismissing his thoughts.

"He's not a myth. He needs me, Dad. I want to be with him. He's—"

Her father lifted her chin so she was looking up at him. "We discussed your time on land before you came on this deadly adventure. You were going to keep to yourself while up here, then you'd come home to the water and carry out your duty to your people. *We* need you there, Unna. You said you would go along with your destiny if I granted you this one reprieve. Look at the danger you've gotten yourself wrapped up in." He brushed a wet strand of hair from her face. "I don't want any more insolence from you. You're not welcomed by these people on land. They just want to take advantage of you."

I opened my mouth to reply, but Unna pushed away from her father. It looked like things were about to become heated between the two of them. I didn't want to see them fight, especially not over me, but I wanted Unna in my life.

24

UNNA

I climbed to my feet, albeit a little unsteadily. I couldn't believe my father was trying to argue with me about this. I truly knew what I wanted for the first time in my life. How could he be telling me no now? I knew I had obligations to my people, but they'd never been what I wanted in my life. Not if it meant sacrificing my happiness and turning into an empty shell. I wanted more from life than that. I lifted my chin a little, knowing I was being defiant to the one person I'd never challenged before, but I had too much to lose now.

My body still felt weak, but I had to be strong. I had to show him I wouldn't back down. I glanced back at Colin, who was watching us carefully. It looked like he was keeping his emotions mostly in check, but his eyes were wolf amber. The effect was stunning, even if it was also a little scary. He was the big bad wolf that I cared for. I knew he needed me as much as I needed him.

"It's not insolence, Father. I'm not being taken advantage of, either. Not by Colin." I walked the few steps to him and sat by his side. Colin wrapped his arm around my shoulders, and the moment he did, I knew from the bottom of my heart that everything was going to be okay. We would make it through this. I wasn't scared anymore that our relationship wouldn't work. It would. "He means a lot to me. He's saved me from the others and been my protector."

"Ægir tried to help you. You pushed him away, and this man nearly killed him." My father frowned and looked between us. "Do you want to explain why you didn't accept Ægir's help?"

I squeezed my hands into fists in my lap. "I didn't need his help. Ægir tried to start a fight with Colin, and Colin felt like he was a threat to me. He was defending me."

"He nearly killed your mate is what he did, and you're hanging all over him."

"No. Ægir isn't my mate, Father. I think you know that as well as I do. He could never be the one for me. He's too full of himself. I don't want to have a selkie husband just for extending our family line. I want what you and mother had. I want something real. Is that too much to ask?" I leaned into Colin, breathing in his scent through the smell of the sea water. Ægir might hold out hope for us, but he didn't make me feel what Colin did.

"No, it's not too much to ask. However—"

I shook my head. "Please. I'm cold and tired. I need to rest."

My father sighed. "We will talk later. Ægir has told me where the werewolf resides. Remain here a moment. I'll return." I opened my mouth to protest, but he slid the rest of the way into his sealskin and once more shifted into his true form. He moved to the edge of the boat and slid into the water gracefully.

Colin ran his hand over my arm. "Thank you."

"Don't thank me for that. I meant every word I said." I looked up at him and smiled. "I care about you. I...love you."

He brushed the hair away from my face and pressed a kiss against my lips that held all the passion I could handle and more. Desire stirred within my belly, but this wasn't the time or place. Nearly dying had set my priorities in order, though. More than ever, I needed Colin's love, and I needed to settle down someplace I could call my own.

"I—"

A splash brought our attention back to the edge of the boat, and a loud seal bark made me climb to my feet to see what was going on. That was my father's commanding tone. I'd know it anywhere. But I had to admit I was happy to hear it, happy to see him again, even if we were arguing about my future. This moment meant more to me now than it would have before. Nearly being taken against my will and killed really changed things.

I looked over the side of the boat to see him carefully carrying my pelt in his mouth. Farther from the boat two bodies floated in the water, but I focused in on my father not wanting to think about what had happened to Murray and his friend. I started to climb over the side to dive into the water, but Colin grabbed me by the waist.

"What are you doing?" he asked. His breath was coming faster now, and a frown creased his lips.

"I'm jumping into the water for my pelt." I had my sealskin back now, and Murray's 'spell' was over. I knew it had been weakened the moment I grabbed my pelt from the storage bench. I didn't feel the same pull to be with him anymore. But there were only two things that could completely break the spell: having my pelt back, or his death. And I technically didn't have it back yet. I chewed on my lower lip, wondering what had happened to Murray.

"I don't feel comfortable with you getting back into the water." He kept his gaze on mine, only dipping his glance to my lips for a moment before staring into my eyes again. "I know your da's down there, but what if you..."

"I'm of the water, Colin. My father's down there. He'll make sure I'm okay." I caressed his cheek. "Don't worry."

"I do worry. I worry that once you have your pelt back, you'll swim away and I'll never see you again. I couldn't bear that." He pressed his forehead against mine. "Tell me you won't disappear on me."

"I..." I froze, unable to speak for a moment. "I won't disappear." But I wasn't sure if I would have the strength to come back and stay on land once I had my pelt. I wrapped my arms around his chest and leaned into him. "I'll see you again."

He held me close, his grip tight, and for a moment I didn't think he'd let me go. But he did. "Fine. Go then. We'll see one another again." He didn't look like he believed me completely, but he pressed a soft kiss to my lips before walking away.

My heart hurt to see him turn around and leave. I nearly opened my mouth to tell him not to go, but another loud bark from my father made me turn back to him. I jumped into the water, slipped into the pelt, and dove underwater to swim home and say goodbye to my pod.

25

COLIN

*W*hile I knew I should've made sure she got into the water fine, I couldn't watch her leave. My eyes burned a little from unshed tears, but I managed to hold them back. My time in Durness was coming to a close. I had booked the cottage for longer, but I couldn't see myself staying on. Between the men who escaped the boat and the memories of Unna, I just couldn't be here. Besides, my wolf and I were both feeling the hurt. Perhaps our love and loss had finally put us on the same path.

A road I didn't want to travel again, but we'd been through a lot together now. What I had thought would drive me over the edge now pulled me back from it. I leaned my head back against the driver's seat, then turned the keys in the ignition. It'd been a while since I'd checked my mobile, which I'd turned off. I cared about my sister, but I hadn't wanted to talk to her, nor did I want to speak with Dougal or Chad. Unfortunately, now I had to go back to reality.

The drive back to the pub was a lonely one. I hadn't realized just how much I enjoyed being around Unna. I knew I cared for her, but now I realized her presence in and of itself was soothing. She just radiated a light that I'd never seen before. Something about her was magical.

I pushed open the door and Mike waved at me. He looked behind me and then back at my face. "Where's the lass?" he asked.

"Her vacation ended. She's gone back home now." I handed him the keys. "It's in the parking spot where you left it." I retreated from the bar, not really wanting to talk with anyone.

"What? What do you mean, lad?" He came out from around the bar, telling one of the few other employees to man it while he went outside. Then he jogged after me, grabbing my elbow.

I froze up, feeling the slow rise of my beast, but I shoved him down. This time he let me do it easily, which surprised me. I wasn't used to him obeying me. Things had changed after all. "I mean just what I said. She went home."

"Is that why you had to borrow my truck? To drive her to the airport?" He looked skeptical, but I shrugged my shoulders.

"Thanks for lending it to us. Take good care of yourself. I'm going to be heading out of town myself, but I appreciate your kindness." I nodded to him and started walking.

"You're a strange one all right, but you're a good man. Take care, lad." The door closed behind Mike as he went back inside.

The walk back to the cottage was a peaceful one. I started making a list of items I'd need to pack and the things I'd have to do when I got to the cottage. I'd have to call Dougal, for instance. Before I went back to the United States, I'd go back to Edinburgh for some time to catch up with my sister. Finally. Hopefully this time it wouldn't end with someone being hurt or nearly killed, but I wasn't betting on it. It seemed like something was always going wrong in my life. Maybe it was the plight of werewolves.

When I got within sight of the cottage, I frowned at the automobile sitting in the driveway. I didn't know whose car that was. I hadn't seen it with Murray's henchmen, but maybe he had more people trying to get even with me now. I gritted my teeth. Now wasn't the time for this. I huffed out a breath, ready to tear off heads.

I made my way to the cottage, being careful to scout the area out first. However, either no one was there, or they were excellent at hiding. A hand tapped my shoulder, and I twirled, my fist reaching out to clench around the intruder's throat.

My sister leapt away with the grace of a cat as she grinned at me, but a slight wince creased the corners of her eyes. "Aye, ye haven't changed much. So tense." She frowned after a moment. "Nae, something's happened. What's wrong, Colin?"

I let out a long breath, relieved but also pissed that she was here. I'd come here to get away from it all, not to play hide and seek. "What the bloody hell are ye doin' here, Caitlyn?"

"I asked first." She crossed her arms over her chest. I knew that look. When she used it, she usually ended up with what she wanted.

I looked around to see if I could spot Dougal, her mate and the Alpha of the Scottish Pack. I didn't see him, but that didn't mean he wasn't around. He could be in my cottage. I clenched my hands into fists. He was my Alpha, though. I couldn't get too pissed at him, even if he was sleeping with my sister now.

"It's a long story. You shouldn't have come all this way. When a man goes off, he expects some privacy." I wasn't that angry at her, though. Some part of me was kind of glad for her company now, especially since Unna wasn't here.

"Aye, but the typical brother doesn't leave his unconscious sister in the care of a Pack of unfamiliar werewolves." She cocked an eyebrow at me, and I ran a hand through my hair. A slow growl rumbled my chest, but I knew she was right. It hadn't been good of me to leave her alone with them, and I regretted abandoning her. But if I hadn't left, I would've been just as much of a danger to her. Besides, I knew a werewolf who would've parted heaven and earth for her. While Dougal shouldn't have put the moves on her, he was loyal to a fault.

"You were fine, we both know that. Now what are you doing here?"

She chewed on her lower lip. "I know ye went away because of what happened. I've been worried about you, but...there's some trouble at home in Edinburgh. Dougal sent me for you. Ye may not be his favorite person right now, but you care about me and the Pack."

That threw me off. I couldn't believe things had fallen apart so quickly. What was going on back in Edinburgh? "Why didn't you call?" I asked.

Caitlyn frowned at me. "As ye darn well should know, I tried calling several times over the span of the last few days, but ye never answered." She ran a hand through her hair and nibbled on her lower lip. It reminded me a little of Unna when she was nervous, but I brushed the thought aside.

Don't think about her. She was off with her people, doing her duty. She'd complained about her father's lecture and her role amongst her people, but things were the way they were, and the sooner I came to accept that the better. It was time for me to move on with my life, and if things really had gone downhill with the Scottish Pack, maybe it was for the best that she wasn't here. At least this way she wouldn't find herself in yet another mess that I might not be able to protect her from.

"Right," I said, finally breaking the lingering silence. "I'm sorry. I should've left a way for you to contact me." I looked up at her and frowned. "How did you find me?"

She smiled, but it wasn't especially pleased. "Dougal pulled a few strings, but I remembered that we had come around this area for a trip once when we were younger, with Mother. It made sense that you'd come here to get away." She looked toward the cottage, then back at me again. "The bartender in town said ye were around in these parts, and I let my nose do the rest. While I'm not quite as good a tracker as some of the werewolves, I'm not horrible."

The bartender... Damn. If he'd given my location out to Caitlyn, would he have given it out to Murray and the others? I didn't know what to think, but it was probably a good idea to get out of town now. He had told me information, of course, at the price of buying some drinks. Maybe he was swayed. I couldn't take any chances.

"Well, I'm glad you found me. I need to start packing, then."

"Yes, you do. We're heading out first thing in the morning." She patted my shoulder, then walked toward the cottage without saying another word. I'd expected we'd be leaving now, but her idea made sense. It was dark, and we'd make better time by traveling in the morning. I just didn't like the idea of being here any longer than necessary. Too many memories and heartache.

I followed after her, remembering that the last time I'd entered the cottage had been with Unna. We'd made love on the bed, and with Caitlyn's sensitive nose, I knew she'd be able to smell it. Probably the only reason she didn't smell it on me now was because of my dive into the ocean.

We made it inside, and she looked around the place. She

smiled and nodded. "Nice. If only it didn't smell so heavily of booze and..." She turned and looked at me. "Sex?" She cocked an eyebrow. "Some lovely local girl?"

"N—" Emotion clenched my throat, and I shook my head. Thinking of Unna hurt too much right now. "A lass on vacation. That's all." I turned away from her and started picking up my stuff to pack into my bags. I didn't have a lot of luggage. I'd taken a train up here but driving back would take a lot longer.

"Sounds like an adventure." From the way she said it, I could tell she knew I was hiding something. She always seemed to. "We...uh." She cleared her throat and sat on the couch. "We buried yer father. We dinnae ken when you'd be getting back, so... Aye. It was nice enough, and the Pack was there, minus a few oddballs." She leaned her head forward, staring at the carpet in front of her. "I just thought you'd want to know before we got back."

The monster had abused her and tried to kill her, yet she'd gone to his funeral out of respect for me. I crouched where I was, blown away by the revelation. I'd been so stupid to run off and leave everything and everyone behind. The man was more of a sperm donor than a dad, and yet...

"Thank you." Those two words were all I could summon. I didn't know how to express the gratitude that clenched my chest. I fought an overwhelming need to give her a hug and tell her how sorry I was that I'd failed so badly at being her brother.

"No worries, mate." She looked up at me and gave me the ghost of a smile. "Been through worse than a funeral."

"Aye. Guess you have. Well, I'll get the rest of my things packed. Have ye eaten?" My brogue thickened with my emotions. "I could fix us something." I didn't have much on hand, but after earlier and probably with her long drive, anything would be better than nothing.

"Nae, I haven't. Dinnae fash about cooking. I can." She hopped up from the couch as if she had springs for legs. "Just go on and pack."

"Thanks." I gathered up all my things and did a quick tidying of each room to the best of my ability. As anxious as I was about my sister being here because something was going wrong within the Pack, my thoughts were consumed by Unna. I'd have enough time to face reality when we were on our way to Edinburgh. For now, in Durness, I could still daydream about the what-ifs and might-have-beens.

A knock on the front door jarred me from my thoughts, and I looked up to see Caitlyn standing still at the stove. She looked at me and frowned. "Expecting anyone?"

"No, I'm not." Hope rose up within my chest, but I squashed it just as fast. I'd be an idiot to think it could be her, but no one else really knew where I was. Except for the bartender, and most likely now Murray's flunkies. "Stay back. I'll take a look to see who it is."

Caitlyn frowned at me, giving me a questioning glare. "I may not be fully healed, but I'm not a weakling, Colin. Don't ye even think of me as such."

I shook my head. "Nae, I wouldn't do ye that disservice after all you've done for me, sis. Just hang back a little."

She turned off the stove, then walked past me toward the bedroom. "Fine. But if I hear anything confrontational, I'm not going to have you standing alone."

"All right." I made a mental note to keep my voice down, since I knew she'd be trying to listen in. When I heard the door shut behind her, I continued toward the front door. Just before I could answer, there came another knock on it. This one was a little softer than the first.

I opened the door and saw Unna and her father standing on the doorstep. My jaw fell open for a second before I could close it. "Hello." I kept my tone neutral, doing my best not to throw my arms around her and memorize her body with my hands. I knew we wouldn't work together, but I didn't want to try to be apart.

"Hi." She smiled at me, and it warmed my heart a little, chipping off some of the ice that had formed after she'd taken off at the docks.

"Do you want to let us in, werewolf?" Her father looked at me expectantly. I hated that they'd be coming in where Caitlyn could easily listen, but I didn't really have any other choice.

"Sure. Make yourself at home." I stepped out of the way, but I kept my gaze mostly fixed on Unna. "I didn't expect to see you back here."

Unna frowned at me, but when her father looked in our direction, she returned her expression to a more neutral one. "Of course I'm here. I told you I'd see you again."

I bit back my response. Just because she'd said it didn't mean she'd meant it. I'd been hurt before by others. Sometimes women didn't always say what they meant. The fact she was a selkie woman made things even more complicated. How would we be together if she was tied to the ocean?

"My daughter keeps her word." Her father looked at her, frowning a little. There seemed to be a private exchange between them, and I wondered what that meant.

"I didn't realize I'd meet someone like him while on land, Father. Colin is...so much more than I'd ever thought I could have. He's my future." Unna smiled at me.

"Seven years. That's how long you'll have before she needs to come home and sire pups with Ægir." Her father propped his hands on his hips, looking authoritative. Like a king...or an Alpha.

I frowned and looked between the two of them. "Seven years? But—"

"No. She will come back to me at that time. I will not accept her mad notion of staying on land if that isn't in place. She is bound by the ocean's call. After seven years, I will come for her, and you will have to say your good-byes, once and for all."

The idea of spending seven years with her sounded blissful, but losing her after we'd gotten closer and fallen harder for one another killed me. Yet... I was between a rock and a hard place. If we did this, we could be buying ourselves time to figure out how to break the spell. I just hoped we could.

When I returned to the United States, I had just the person in mind to ask: Mia, the witch who had helped to free me and the others from the research facility. While some of the Southeastern Pack still hated her for poisoning the Alpha, Chad had told us that she hadn't done so on purpose.

"Fine." I looked to Unna. "What do you say, love?"

She smiled for the first time since she'd come inside the cottage, and nodded. "Yes."

"Then I grant you this." Her father handed over a sturdy case to me. It looked like a small safe of some kind. I frowned, but reluctantly accepted it. "It's her pelt. With this, you will be her human husband, caretaker of her, lover of her. If I find out that you've harmed a hair on her head, you are as good as dead."

I heard a small noise from the bedroom, and I did my best not to react to it. Once her father left, I'd have to explain to her what was going on and that we were leaving. Actually, I should probably tell him that part now.

"I swear not to hurt her. We will be leaving first thing in the morning, though. We need to visit Edinburgh on some important business."

She frowned at me and then looked to her father. "I'll

miss you, Dad. Take care of everyone, and especially yourself. I promise to visit and send messages through Ailsa."

He nodded, and the authoritative figure in front of me melted, to be replaced by a concerned father. He pulled Unna into his arms and gave her a big hug. Tears shone in his eyes, but he didn't let them fall. For a moment, jealousy welled within me. She had the one thing I'd always hoped for. My own father was a major asshole. It would've been great to have someone like her dad around. But I guess what she lacked, I had...for the most part.

My mother was good, but at times she lived in her own world. When Caitlyn and I had come of age, she'd gone off to mainland Europe with some Swedish model she'd met. They seemed to be happy enough, but she rarely called or wrote, at least not to me. I wasn't sure if Caitlyn kept in touch with her, but I kind of doubted it.

We sent Christmas cards, and she sometimes mailed postcards from the different places she traveled, but that was about all. She'd done her job with raising us, but we weren't her problem anymore.

I shrugged those thoughts aside, knowing I needed to come back to the present. "I'll help her with whatever she needs."

Her father nodded to me, then spoke to her in their language. She hugged him tightly and said something back to him. Tears ran down her face, and she kissed him on the cheek, then turned to me. "I'm excited to go with you to Edinburgh. I've never been to a large city before."

I didn't imagine she had, if she'd only been to the Faroe Islands and here. Edinburgh wasn't even the biggest city there was, but there would probably be some culture shock in her future. "I'll show you around." I smiled at her. "I'm sure we'll have some fun." Another soft bang in the bedroom reminded me again of Caitlyn, and I sighed. "Come on out, sis."

Unna and her father looked to one another in surprise. She frowned, then looked back at me. "I didn't know you had anyone else with you. You were alone earlier, when we were..."

I nodded, then turned to look at Caitlyn as she walked into the room. She cocked an eyebrow at me. "Hello. Looks like ye've been busy since I last saw ye," Caitlyn said, shoving her hands into her pockets. She had a slightly amused look on her face, but I could tell something was going on behind her eyes. She was trying to be friendly, but maybe she was bothered by the fact that I'd met Unna while I was up here. I was sure we'd talk about it later when we got a chance. For now, I had to get everyone on the same page, and that meant figuring this out with Unna and her father before I lost her again.

"Yes, she came up here to get me since she was concerned about me." I glanced over at Caitlyn, who nodded just the slightest bit. We'd used these same discreet glances when we'd been younger and were working together to stay out of trouble with our mother.

"Right. But it's time to come home. Everyone misses you. So, we'll be heading off in my...uh...boyfriend's car tomorrow." She frowned and rolled her shoulders a little. I wondered what that was about, but I didn't dare ask now.

"A road trip? That sounds like fun." Unna turned her frown into a smile and showed the happy expression to her father. "It'll be okay, Dad. I promise."

"Don't make promises you can't keep," he said. "But if you need anything at all, you let Ailsa know. If you want to come home early, we can make that happen." He might've been talking to her, but he looked directly at me when he said it. I knew that selkies had some warriors in their ranks, but I doubted they could take on a Pack of werewolves if we were prepared for the assault. However, I thought enough of myself to know if she did feel like leaving, I wasn't one to force her to stay.

"If she wants to leave me, I wouldn't stop her. I care enough about her to make sure she gets what she wants, regardless of how I feel about it." I looked over to the stove, where Caitlyn's dinner was starting to cool again. "Sorry, but we still have things to do before the trip tomorrow. Caitlyn was in the process of cooking supper, if you want to join us."

Her father shook his head. "No, I'll leave you to it." He turned to Unna. "Good-bye, my daughter." Then he said a few things in their language and walked toward the door.

Emotions swept over her face. I could tell this was hard for her. A couple of tears trailed down her cheeks, but she brushed them away.

"I'll finish up dinner, Colin." Caitlyn patted my shoulder, then headed into the adjoining room, leaving me and Unna in pseudo-privacy.

"Are you sure about this?" I asked Unna, brushing my thumb across her cheek and catching another falling tear.

"Yes. I am. I knew it was what I wanted before when we talked, and I...I guess I'm just scared." She wrapped her arms around my waist and rested her head against my chest.

"It'll work out, lass. I know it will." I pressed a kiss to the top of her head. "Where are your things?" For the first time, I noticed that she didn't have a bag with her. Maybe it was still at the selkies' cottage, but somehow I didn't think so. I also saw that her clothes seemed too big for her petite frame, and they didn't exactly match, either. Like they weren't hers.

She chewed on her lower lip and lowered her gaze, not meeting my eyes. "I...I don't have anything."

The reality of her words hit me hard. I wanted to provide for her. To love and care for her. To protect her. She was my woman, and I couldn't let her go around without anything, even if I wasn't exactly rolling in cash.

"I can take her shopping, if she'd like." I looked over to see Caitlyn leaning against the entryway to the living room. "Food's ready."

Unna looked up at Caitlyn, then at me. "That would be very kind of you." She pulled back a little. "Hi, I'm Unna."

Caitlyn walked toward us and held out her hand. "Hello, Unna. I'm Caitlyn." She nodded, then turned and disappeared back into the kitchen. I heard the clink of silverware as she went about preparing our plates.

"Our future might not be easy. There's trouble among the people Caitlyn is with now. Trouble I walked away from to come here." I brushed a strand of blonde hair from her face. "I'll do my best to protect you, but we're diving into more danger, not running from it. I just don't want you to expect things to be less dangerous than they are now."

She rose to her tiptoes and kissed me on the lips. "I know that if I'm with you then danger is the least of my concerns. You saved my future and my life here. I don't know how I can begin to repay you for that."

"Just be with me and love me." I returned her kiss, brushing my lips against hers. Suddenly, dinner wasn't even something I cared about. I just wanted to be inside Unna again. My heart rejoiced at being near her. Only Caitlyn clearing her throat brought me back to the present. "Let's eat, then we can...get some sleep." I smirked down at Unna and winked.

Her eyes widened, then a grin curved her lips. "I'd like that very much."

"Well, ye two love birds will need to wait. The food is going to get cold if you keep kissing," Caitlyn said from the other room.

There was definitely something going on with her. I just

wasn't sure what it was yet. It put a little bit of a damper on my desire for Unna, but not enough of one to diminish my joy of her being here with me, knowing I would have her in my bed later. For now, I'd bide my time. I'd figure out what was going on soon.

Ready for more Cry Wolf? Grab the fifth book, *The Leopard Who Claimed A Wolf...*

AUTHOR'S NOTE

Thank you for reading *The Selkie Who Loved A Wolf*. I hope you enjoyed it!

It was a pleasure hopping back into the Cry Wolf series. Getting into Colin's head was both fun and challenging. He's an intense guy who went through a lot. While he and Unna don't have a happily ever after right now, they are on the right path to one. The next book will return to Caitlyn and Dougal and the problems going on within the Scottish Pack.

Please consider leaving a review at the retailer's website or on Goodreads, even if it's a line or two. It truly helps!

If you're interested in being the first to know about my next release, sign up for my newsletter.

ABOUT THE AUTHOR

New York Times & USA Today Bestselling Author Sarah Mäkelä loves her fiction dark, magical, and passionate. She is a paranormal romance author and a life-long paranormal fan who still sleeps with a night light. In her spare time, she reads sexy books, watches scary movies, and plays computer games with her husband. When she gets the chance, she loves traveling the world too.

amazon.com/author/sarahmakela

bookbub.com/authors/sarah-makela

instagram.com/authorsarahmakela

facebook.com/authorsarahmakela

twitter.com/sarahmakela

goodreads.com/sarahmakela

pinterest.com/authorsarahmakela

ALSO BY SARAH MÄKELÄ

Currently Available for Free *

Cry Wolf Series

(New Adult Paranormal Romance)

Book 1: The Witch Who Cried Wolf *

Book 2: Cold Moon Rising

Book 3: The Wolf Who Played With Fire

Book 4: Highland Moon Rising

Book 5: The Selkie Who Loved A Wolf

Book 6: The Leopard Who Claimed A Wolf

Cry Wolf Series Boxed Set (Books 1-3)

Beneath the Broken Moon Serial

(New Adult Paranormal Romance)

Part 1 *

Part 2

Part 3

Part 4

Part 5

Season One (Parts 1-5)

Edge of Oblivion

Book 1: The Assassin's Mark

Book 2: The Thief's Gambit

The Amazon Chronicles Series

(New Adult Paranormal Romance)

Book 1: Jungle Heat

Book 2: Jungle Fire

Book 3: Jungle Blaze

Book 4: Jungle Burn

The Amazon Chronicles Collection

Hacked Investigations Series

(Futuristic Paranormal Romance)

Book 1: Techno Crazed

Book 2: Savage Bytes

Book 2.5: Internet Dating for Gnomes *

Book 3: Blacklist Rogue

Book 4: Digital Slave

Courts of Light and Dark

(New Adult Fantasy Romance)

Book 1: Captivated

Book 2: Surrendered

Standalones

Moonlit Feathers

Captive Moonlight

Vera's Christmas Elf

EXCERPT FOR THE LEOPARD WHO CLAIMED A WOLF (CRY WOLF #6)

CAITLYN

The driveway leading up to the Scottish Pack's massive headquarters stretched almost half a mile. I rested my chin on my arms and stared out of the Alpha's window on the second story, overlooking the circular section of the drive. The Pack's castle came complete with its very own dungeon, but at least they weren't keeping me in there anymore. The memory of Alistair's craggy face haunted my dreams each time I closed my eyes. His brutal fists hammered away against my face, ribs, and stomach, until I could no longer sleep.

Tension radiated through my shoulders, and I balled my hands into fists. No, Alistair—Colin's father—was dead. Dougal had protected me, and my brother, from that monster when I didn't have the strength to fight back.

Not that it mattered.

Two days had passed since my brother's sudden departure. Now Colin was on his own with no one to watch his back. How could he leave without saying anything to me? I flexed my fists again, welcoming the anger as it bubbled up in my chest and replaced my sadness.

The heavy weight of a man's hand descended on my back. I twisted around, my knuckles connecting with a solid jaw lined with dark, coarse stubble. A familiar jaw. *Shite.*

Dougal stumbled back half a step, but then he planted his feet like a tree with strong roots, not budging any further. Sharp power flared outward from him before he squelched it, stretching the muscles in his jaw. A frown tugged at his lips, and the corners of his eyes creased, either in pain or displeasure.

"Dougal! I'm so sorry." The sudden movement of punching him had shot a searing ache through my battered ribs again. The pain stole my breath away, but I tried to force it down. How could I have been so careless? If he'd been anyone else in the Pack, I would've caused World War III.

"Dinnae fash. The punch bloody well hurt, though. I didn't realize you were so strong." Dougal's frown melted away as he pulled me closer and pressed a kiss to my forehead. "Seems like you're recovering your strength." His gaze drifted past me to the long gravel driveway of the estate. "How are you doing, love?"

The emotions I'd been stomping down now bubbled to the surface again. "I cannae believe Colin left me. He left before I even regained consciousness. How could he?" With anyone else, I wouldn't show weakness, but I rested my forehead against Dougal's chest, needing his touch and savoring his warmth. "I barely had time to talk with him, and when I did, it wasn't a good time to ask how he was doing after the months he'd spent in that bloody research facility— or even to ask where he would go to heal…"

Tears welled in my eyes, but I held them back, refusing to cry. "I gave up so much—my job, my flat, my life—while trying to track him and bring him home. What if my sacrifices were all for naught?"

"Nae, they weren't for naught, love." Dougal kissed the

top of my head. "I know you're hurting. You have plenty of reasons to be, but the man who came back wasn't the same one who left for the United States." He lifted my chin, forcing me to see the sincerity in his clear blue eyes. "Whatever those scientists did affected him in ways neither of us will probably ever know. Waiting at the window won't make him return any sooner." He wrapped his arms around me and gently pulled me against his chest again. "Let me draw you a bath. Remember, I'm here if you need to talk."

He was right, even if I didn't want to admit it. Waiting for Colin's return wouldn't help, but what else could I do? "I know, but that doesn't make this any easier for me. He's my younger brother. I feel helpless that I cannae be there for him...again." A heavy ache settled on my heart, and I pulled away hating the awkward emotions crushing me. "Sorry."

Dougal turned away from me and stared out of the window again. His jaw clenched and unclenched, as if he were trying hard to hold in his words. A lot was going on in his life too, and yet he was making a strong effort to support me through my problems. Things had become increasingly strained between him and his Pack since my arrival and Duncan and Alistair's subsequent deaths. He didn't talk about what he faced, and I didn't want to pressure him.

After a few moments of silence, he released a sigh and turned back toward me. "You've done what you could for him, lass." The ghost of a grin spread across his lips. "Do you still want the bath?"

I couldn't help but nod. When I'd awakened from unconsciousness, Dougal had been there for me. We'd made love, and he brought me to new heights of pleasure. We also became intimately acquainted with the fancy Jacuzzi bathtub that could easily fit three or four humans...or one big, scary werewolf. The perks of being mated to the Alpha of the Scottish Pack.

"Aye, a bath sounds delish." I wrapped my arms around his waist, bringing him back to me and drawing in his musky lupine scent. "Thanks for the talk. I wish I could've spoken with him before he took off. It would've made me feel better about him going."

"Love, I talked with him." He trailed his fingertips over my back in light, soothing strokes. "If I weren't confident that he presented no danger to others, I wouldn't have let him go. He would've stayed here whether he favored the idea or not." The muscles in his lower back tensed beneath my touch, and his hand paused over my spine.

Something didn't feel right. I lifted my gaze to meet Dougal's. Was he not telling me something? We hadn't known each other for long, but my sharp, feline instincts knew when someone spoke an untruth. He wasn't outright lying, but he was holding something back. What could it be?

I bit my lower lip, regretting it as my teeth sank into one of the nearly healed spots where Alistair had punched me in the face. Instead of confronting Dougal, I turned my attention toward the window. "You would tell me if he was dangerous to himself, wouldn't you?"

"Aye, I would." His tone of voice wasn't as convincing as I'd wanted. He leaned away, putting me at arm's length. "Enough of that, I suppose. I'll draw the bath for you." Without another word, he strode to the en-suite bathroom. His hands clenched and unclenched at his sides all the way. The door snapped shut behind him, and he started the water running a few moments later.

Nausea churned inside me, and I held my stomach. Should I believe Dougal? Something about his words didn't feel right. The Jacuzzi tub would take a few minutes to fill, and I needed to get out of this bloody bedroom and away from him. The strain of standing there and trying to keep myself calm was becoming too much.

My stomach growled, and I glanced up at the round wrought-iron clock on the wall. It was almost one o'clock in the afternoon.

Many of the werewolves didn't like that their Alpha was mating with a wereleopard, so I usually skipped the mealtime rushes to keep my distance. It wasn't easy, because several of the wolves lived here in this honest-to-God castle full time. Apparently, that was how many Packs operated. The thought boggled my mind. How did they stand to be around one another all the time? How would I survive being the sole feline in this house full of wolves?

Every urge for solitude within me roared to run as fast and as far away from this place as I could. Too much held me here, though. Besides, if Colin returned from his trip, I wanted to be around to greet him. Maybe throttle him, too, but it'd be a greeting nonetheless…

I slid my leather jacket on over the white tank top, not wanting to reveal too much bruised skin, then headed for the kitchen to grab leftovers. Dougal had tried to convince me to eat with him and everyone else. He wanted me to get to know the wolves and socialize. Getting friendly with the Pack might be a nice idea, but I couldn't do it. Not with how his Pack watched me when they thought I wasn't looking. Even Dougal's second-in-command wasn't a fan of mine. The sentiment was mutual. For as long as I could remember, I'd hated werewolves. One of my main reasons would soon rest six feet underground. Their hatred of me for Alistair's death just added to my reluctance to get friendly with them.

Shaking away those thoughts, I turned the corner to enter the kitchen. If my sharp feline reflexes hadn't kicked in, I would've run straight into a towering werewolf. I leapt back at the last minute to prevent Kerr from spilling his plate of food. The already agonizing ache in my side intensified from moving so fast, but I kept my arms at my sides and my face neutral.

"Afternoon, lass. Ye look like yer recoverin' well." Kerr nodded, looking curiously at me.

"Thanks, Kerr. I'm trying." I flashed him an uncomfortable smile, then edged past the broad, barrel-chested man into the kitchen. Maybe he wasn't as bad as the others, but I couldn't shake the overwhelming feeling that he disagreed with Dougal's decision to mate with me.

Kerr placed a heavy hand on my shoulder. My spine stiffened, and I gripped the sleeves of my jacket to keep from swinging on him too. "Keep tryin', then." His deep voice rumbled through the kitchen. I glanced pointedly at his hand, but he didn't move it. "Sooner or later ye need to overcome yer fear, hatred, or whatever it is ye feel toward my kind. If ye cannae, ye won't last long here, lass." With that, he walked down the corridor toward the massive grand hall where the wolves held their meetings and ate.

My shoulders slumped. Suddenly, I didn't feel so hungry, but my leopard still needed to eat. We couldn't skip any more meals. It hindered our healing process and weakened us too much. Right now, I couldn't afford weakness, not while I was amongst a pack of wolves.

If only I weren't continually looking over my shoulder with the Pack, but such was life for now.

Shite. I didn't have much time before Dougal noticed I'd left the bedroom.

The leftovers were neatly arranged on the clean countertop. There wasn't much food left, but I grabbed a bag of crisps and one of the last club sandwiches. A female wolf —Mairi, I think—ran a catering company, so she always brought by food to keep the Pack well fed. She was one of the nicer wolves.

Instead of following Kerr toward the dining room, where

I would probably find the rowdy werewolves laughing and talking, I remained in the kitchen. I sat on the counter farthest away from the entrance, hidden from anyone who might walk past.

As I finished my sandwich, footsteps in the hall became louder as someone approached the kitchen. The sound of soft sniffing tensed every muscle in my body, then Dougal stepped into the room. His gaze slid over me, and desire darkened his eyes.

"Your bath is ready. If I'd known you were hungry, I would've brought something earlier when I ate."

I shrugged a shoulder. "It's all right. I'm eating now."

"Aye, so you are." He looked down the hallway as if checking to make sure no one else was near. When he turned back, he wore a frown that creased the corners of his lips and eyes. "You shouldn't be in here all alone, love. Things within the Pack are tense right now. Let's go back to the bedroom."

I tilted my chin up, not in the mood to be bossed around again. "I'm not alone. You're here." I opened the bag of crisps and munched on one.

His nostrils flared, and he crossed his arms over his broad chest. The move might've been scary as hell if it wasn't him doing it. "That's not the point. Come on."

Bloody hell.

First, I'd been his prisoner in the cage, and now I'd become a prisoner in his bedroom. Not in a fun way, either. Why was this happening?

I clenched my fists, crushing a few of my crisps as tears burned in my eyes, but I refused to let them show. The flood of emotions I'd experienced over the past week was becoming too much to all push down at once. As soon as I dealt with certain fears or emotions, others popped up to take their place, like some horrible version of whack-a-mole.

Life just wasn't fair. All I'd wanted to do was return to

Scotland and be here for my brother. In that time, I'd been reintroduced to a childhood nightmare, imprisoned in a dungeon, and now I was the prisoner/mate of a werewolf Alpha. When would the roller coaster end?

Dougal crossed the space between us in a few long strides. He pulled me from the counter into his arms.

A feline hiss ripped from my throat, sounding every bit as feral as I felt. Once again, anger rescued me from my moodiness. "Set me down this minute!"

59068672R00104